VERMONT BRIDE

War Time Romance Collection
Book #2

By
Marlene Bierworth

Disclaimer

This book is a work of fiction, based on a true event. Although the story is based on history, many names, places, character and twist of events are the product of the author's imagination. While the author has tried to be historically correct, her goals in this book are to create great characters and tell a love story. Fictional characters have been introduced into the event surrounding the St. Albans Raid in Vermont, with the sole intention of publishing an entertaining fictional book. Any resemblance to actual persons, living or dead, events or locals, is purely coincidental.

ABOUT THE BOOK

A northern farmgirl, Emma Miller, and an injured southern soldier, William Davis, come together unexpectedly, never imagining romance to spark between them and take them on a whirlwind adventure readers will not soon forget.

When thirty gentlemen show up in St. Albans over the span of a week, spending money and interacting with the locals, the town lets down their guard to welcome a bit of normal life amidst deep unrest in the country.

Are things as they seem, or is there a deceptive plan underfoot?

Help cheer on this fragile romance and see if love can survive during wartime. Pick up this historical, inspirational, novella today!

All the books in this series are standalone romance stories set during different war times in history. See all the books in this series here:

https://www.amazon.com/gp/product/B08BRX6TS7

ABOUT THE TIMES

The Civil War began on April 12, 1861 and ended on April 9, 1865. It started when the Confederates attacked Union soldiers at Fort Sumpter, South Carolina. Tensions had been rising for years, however, in the course of a day, history was forever altered.

The war pitted brother against brother, and family against family. It crossed all social, economic, race, and gender lines. Very few were untouched during these years. Major cities became equipment suppliers, and women assumed jobs previously held by their husbands, fathers or brothers. It was a terrible time in American history and the bloodiest battle fought on American soil in which over 60,000 men perished.

NOTE: Although this is primarily a love story, there was nothing romantic about the Civil War. **Marlene Bierworth, however, has chosen to focus on the romance and tension between two individuals with war in the background. This love story does not attempt to take on the format of historical accuracy to the letter, but includes fictional characters interacting within the backdrop of unrest.**

TABLE OF CONTENTS

Chapter 1

ETHAN COMES HOME

The steps from the underground cold cellar were steep as Emma climbed the wooden rungs to the kitchen. Weighing heavy on her arm hung a pail of garden vegetables which included carrots, onions, turnips, and potatoes, but the loose hem of her shabby dress constantly caught underfoot and threatened to send her tumbling back to the dirt floor below. She should have worn her work trousers, but this was Papa's birthday and she wanted to dress nicely for him. Tonight, she'd prepare his favourite meal—roast pork—surrounded by a mountain of vegetables with chili relish on the side to help brighten his mood. While he'd worked the north field yesterday, Emma had baked a cake. The after-dinner surprise would please him. She'd even attempt to sing Mama's birthday ditty that he loved to hear and manage the groan on cue when he clapped out of tune, just as she'd done at every birthday since a child. For one captivating moment, they would taste joy from the past and rejoice.

The date was October 10th, 1864, and there was little to celebrate in St. Albans, Vermont. The Civil War had occupied the entire country for nearly three-and-a-half years, leaving America to suffer vile devastation, the likes of which tormented Emma's dreams every single night. Nothing made sense anymore. Victory and defeat both muddled in pools of dirty water inside her head. One out of every nine eligible men in her state had marched off to war hoping to stop the Rebel traitors.

What did any of it matter anymore? Two of her brothers lay on some backwoods battleground where birds of prey picked at their remains and bones sunk into unfriendly soil. One remained alive; Ethan, but she hadn't heard from him in a long time.

"Daughter! Come quick," Joseph Miller shouted overhead. "Riders coming."

Her nerves peaked—one could never be too cautious these days. She'd ascended the makeshift ladder too far now to go back with the precious contents of the pail. As Emma topped the final step, she met her father's frantic eyes.

"Relax, Papa. It may be the Union soldiers—perhaps even Ethan coming home." That appeared to soften the lines of dread etched in his face.

"Good thinking, girl." He snatched the pail and set it on the floor, then offered a hand to help her over the top and into the kitchen. "Grab hold of the mat and let's get this hole covered – just in case."

The hinged section of the floor fell into place and they straightened the oval braided rug over the top. Placing the family table strategically in the middle hid the cellar entrance from the many two-footed scavengers that roamed the woods. The bountiful harvests of root produce and smoked meat needed to see them through the winter.

At the window, they watched the laneway for the first sign of a rider. Emma breathed easier when the blue suits came into view, although after years of weather, the color had paled and lost its shine. Some soldiers had given up wearing uniforms altogether and fought battles in pants and shirts they stole off a woman's clothesline along their travels.

Emma's voice rose with excitement. "Look, Papa. It's James, riding upfront." She raced to the door. "Ethan must be with them."

Her enthusiasm died when Captain James Fitzpatrick did not attempt to crack a smile at the sight of her running toward him. They'd known one another since first grade and he'd always called her his best girl. Fear slowed her steps, and she halted six feet from the lead horse. Emma's gaze trailed to the mount connected to the end of the rope James held firmly between his white-knuckled fingers. Directly behind him, she saw Blaze, the mare who had survived all the conflicts and lived to carry her owner home. Ethan's body was slung over the saddle and his wrists and feet tied securely to keep him from slipping to the ground.

Emma froze to the spot, staring at what remained of the Miller boys. The wool blue coat Mama had sewn last time he rode through had ripped again, and the bare flesh of his arm peeked through. The crusty blood and open gash made her want to vomit. Not that she was the nauseous type, for she'd seen her share of injuries, both human and animal. She'd just seen far too much of it.

James swung off of his saddle. He dropped to the ground and cautiously approached her. Wrapping a sympathetic arm around her shoulders, he whispered, "His end came quick, Emma. I was grateful for that. Too many soldiers suffer for days then end up dying, anyway."

She looked at him through glassy eyes. "They're all gone. My entire family wiped out."

"Your father—is he all right?" James asked, concern etching the hard lines in his face.

Emma whirled around and noticed her father

on the porch, slumped over like a droopy willow branch, his fingers clinging to the cedar post of the railing to stay upright. She picked up her skirt and ran toward him.

"Papa," she cried as she drew close to the covered porch. Emma sprang up the five steps and gathered him into her arms. He never acknowledged her but hung limply while continuing to stare at Blaze and the heavy load he carried. He shivered, and she moved him to the rocking chair. Falling into it, he buried his head in the palms of his hands. No sound uttered from his lips, just the horrid tremor that shook his body nonstop. She reached for the blanket she'd tossed on the other rocker and wrapped him in it, tucking in the sides and covering his shoulders.

"Pa, don't go to that place again. It's only you and me left. We need each other." Emma tried to sound firm, chiding him as if he were the child and she the adult.

Her plea fell on deaf ears. His vacant eyes lifted, but it seemed too much of a chore to hold his head up and she watched it drop to his chest. A heavy sigh escaped his open mouth and Emma's heart quickened. She'd heard her mother's final breath, and it had sounded much the same as his loud exhale today, but she refused to take stock in such omens. Dropping to her knees, she wrapped strong arms around her father, listening to his ragged breathing while beseeching God to bring them comfort and strength. The soldiers in the yard remained silent as Ethan Miller's father and sister mourned the loss of another family member.

Several minutes passed before James trudged up the stairs. Emma heard every clunk of his heavy boots as it hit the creaking boards, and when he touched her back, she twisted her teary face in his direction. He helped her stand, and she used the hem of her apron to wipe the tears from her swollen eyes.

"Time to bury him, Emma. It's been two days." Emma understood the procedure. "We'll need you to identify him. Army's a stickler on paperwork. The major sends his condolences; said to tell you Ethan was a first-rate trooper and you should be proud that he died for his country."

Emma stared at James strangely, wondering how he'd grown so accustomed to death, even the death of a close friend.

"Those are nice-sounding words, James, but I just wanted him to come home alive." She straightened her countenance and moved clear of James's overprotective ways that always left her craving fresh air. "At least this time we have a body to bury and pray over. That's a sight better than what my other brothers received."

Emma fought to keep her voice from cracking. She'd need to be the anchor for her father, who these days crossed over the edge of sanity far too often.

Emma pushed past James without a backward glance to her now, only living relative. Joseph Miller would be useless to identify his son. He saw ghosts walking every day and called them whatever name suited his frame of mind. She lifted her countenance and walked directly toward Blaze, her eyes never wavering from the saddle. The mare whinnied and nudged Emma. Animals grieved for people—of that she felt certain—for sadness showed in her huge, glassed-over, brown eyes. Emma stroked the long snout and mumbled some soothing words, maybe more for her benefit than for the beast.

Laying her head against Blaze for support, Emma forced her eyes to look up. A blanket covered his face, and with one hand she pulled back the corner. Her heartbeat plummeted to near silence as rivers of tears spilled down her cheeks. "Oh, Ethan. I love you so."

Eventually, James dragged her away. "The men will dig a hole in the family graveyard. We'll call you when it's ready." Emma glanced at the small company of Ethan's comrades still sitting on their mounts. She mustered a weak smile and said, "Thank you." One after another they dismounted while James led her toward the house.

When they reached the bottom step, James cleared his throat. "Sorry to be bothering you at a time like this, but the men haven't eaten today. We have a chunk of deer meat, freshly carved, if you have the strength to cook it for us."

Emma regarded James and answered the only acceptable way. "Certainly. The war goes on and our soldiers need feeding. I'll stoke the fire."

Her sluggish movements caused intense exhaustion, a familiar feeling, and one she knew could be deadly to a grieving heart. Her father remained on the rocker, and with regret she passed him by, leaving him alone to work through his sorrow. There was work to do, and perhaps busy hands would combat the spirit of doom and gloom that had invaded this sixtieth birthday celebration.

She placed a large pot of water on the stove for the vegetables she'd brought from the cellar to make soup. October was chilly and the travelers were undoubtedly weary. Emma decided to save the small cut of pork for another day. They should eat the venison, as the men had no way of keeping it fresh while riding the trails. When James brought it in and slapped it on the counter, Emma nodded.

"It's a good chunk of meat, James. Enough to quiet the hunger pangs of your men outside." He grabbed a knife and sliced it into smaller portions. The feast provided thirty man-size slabs when he finished. He worked in silence, and when finished, left the kitchen.

Emma began to hum two of her favorite hymns repeatedly until the peace filtered through to her aching heart. Creator God was still the King of the mountaintops and His grace surely amazing. He'd walk with them through this ordeal the same as He had in the past. Throughout her childhood, singing had been her mother's cure for everything, but when she'd needed it most, her songs dried up, and she lay curled under bedcovers waiting for the Lord to take her home to heaven. Emma vowed she'd praise His faithfulness as long as He gave her breath.

With a sharp knife, she trimmed away the excess fat and put it with the pile James had cut off. She'd use it to make soap later. The men had done a good job preparing the tenderloin, and it saved time now. The chef in her knew it would have tasted better marinated in spices and oil, but she had no time for such luxury. She combined bacon fat, garlic, and mustard, and after slicing gaps into the meat, drizzled the mixture inside to keep it moist while frying. After gathering all the cast iron skillets that she could find, she placed them on the cooktop to preheat. Her father liked his steak done medium-rare, with the blood-red color showing but not dripping in pools on his plate. Everyone would receive like portions today.

Emma turned her attention to the soup and cut vegetables into small pieces and threw them into the boiling water with rice and all the spices she could find on her meager shelves. She then seasoned both sides of the meat with salt and pepper, and when the oil in the pan was just about to smoke, she added the steaks. It sizzled, and she knew she'd gotten the temperature just right. After four minutes on each side, she slathered the top with butter and transferred them onto a flat pan waiting on the cool side of the stove. Emma repeated the procedure until all the slices of meat lay soaking up the moistness. The steaks were a good inch thick, so she had about ten minutes to throw the rest of the meal together. She stirred the soup and stabbed the carrots with a fork. When it went through, she smiled and ran to the pantry for bread. She'd baked this morning, so there were three loaves to slice for the men. Butter, pickles, bread slices, and jam went in the center of the table.

She hurried to the window, and when she spotted James, she yelled, "Tell the men to bring their place settings. Dinner is nearly ready." Emma glanced toward the hill and saw the gravediggers throw their shovels to the ground. The hole was dug and today she'd bury her last brother.

In the past, Mama had often recited these wise words, "One needs to care for the living before tending to the dead—it's scriptural." But in her wildest imaginings the woman could never have expected that her young daughter would face the stark reality of the present day that made such a task so unbearably daunting.

Regardless, tonight Emma and the men would sing happy birthday to Joseph Miller. They'd watch him blow out the one candle she'd purchased at the mercantile and make a wish, if he had any left inside. Then she'd choke down a tiny piece of the festive birthday cake, all while holding back the river of tears she'd indulge in later tonight in the privacy of her bedroom.

Chapter 2

HOLDING STEADY

The next morning, Emma woke hours before the sun blazed over the eastern horizon. With soldiers bunking in the barn, they'd expect her to offer some kind of meal before they pulled out. She'd worked the entire evening in the kitchen preparing the menu. Many hungry mouths lay snoring just beyond her door and would soon gather at her table to wolf down all of her best efforts. Besides a heartfelt thank you, the Millers would receive no pay for their contribution—and that should suffice—yet lately, it didn't. Weariness governed Emma's heart.

Money was tight for her father donated freely to support war projects. Sacrificing for the better good and the freedom of slaves had sounded so patriotic in the spring of 1861, but much had happened since then; families torn apart, lives ruined, homes destroyed, the stealing, the abuse, and the hatred – she grieved for losses that time could not restore. The country would be a long time healing after the final victory shout sounded throughout the land and all the soldiers trickled home imagining life to resume as before. They'd be shocked – especially in the south, where chaos and savagery ran rampant in communities and on plantations.

Emma chose not to dwell on the future. It was a useless endeavor. She felt the warmth of the rising sun rest on her back as daylight streamed through the window. With the last loaf of bread sliced and bacon frying, she heard the tap on the door and turned to see James stroll in.

"Noticed you were awake. Brought the camp coffee pot to help with the crowd, and after snooping around the henhouse, I found another dozen eggs. Gertrude and her bunch do you a fine service in laying all these delicacies." He chuckled. "You realize that all the men went to bed drooling in anticipation of breakfast? You're a fine cook, Emma. Make some man a good wife when this war is over."

Emma coveted the contents of the basket as James passed her the eggs. All she pictured were the few coins she'd have earned from the mercantile for such a sale. She chided herself for allowing selfishness to steal her joy in serving her countrymen.

Lifting her eyes, James drew her in with a strange intensity, one she'd never encountered in all of their childhood years. She read the unasked question written in his face and her heart froze. Involuntarily, she gasped. Her response surprised him.

Stuttering, James attempted to explain the words he'd not braved to utter aloud, but definitely implied. "Don't look at me like you lost your best friend, Emma. I'm not expecting an answer from you today. Guess I always figured we had an understanding."

"Women do not take kindly to men who presume such things. Especially me, James Fitzpatrick."

"Now I've spoiled your good mood. Forget it." James walked toward the window and peered outside. "Can't guarantee I won't be hauled home on the back of my horse, same as Ethan. You don't need another heartbreak."

"Don't talk nonsense. I'll never forgive you if you don't return, head held high and carrying the Union flag." When Emma noticed the spark of hope in his eye, she feared he'd misinterpreted her concern for his welfare as a romantic interest. "Every widow will line the streets seeking to wed a war hero. And you'll be the top contender for any woman's kitchen."

Emma clutched the basket and turned aside to crack the new supply of eggs. James headed for the door, hat in hand and eyes peeled to the floor, and at the sound of the door closing behind him, she breathed a sigh of relief. Emma liked James—always had. She envisioned him through youthful eyes; a great swimming, fishing and hunting companion, but mostly as Ethan's best friend. Never once had she considered anything else between them.

While existing for over three years in a country ravaged by war, time had oddly passed as moments speeding through the sludge of quicksand; an ongoing mockery for her body and soul. Every waking minute of every day, she spent helping the war effort and keeping the farm up and running for her brother's return. But now, no one would come, and the never-ending task would forever become her responsibility. At eighteen-years-old, Emma stood on the edge of womanhood, a prime age for fellas to show romantic interest. Thankfully, all the eligible male suitors had marched off to war, and their absence in the romance department pleased her, mostly. For the second day, she regretted not wearing chore clothes, and silently swore this touch of femininity would hit the ragbag as soon as the soldiers pulled out.

Emma moved to the foot of the stairs and yelled for her father. It wasn't like him to sleep in. But he needed rest, and the longer he stayed under the covers, the better. Yesterday's news fatigued him, both mentally and physically, and she feared for his well-being.

"Papa, come get your coffee before the men empty the pot."

He promptly arrived in the kitchen, fully washed and dressed. "Been waiting for your call, Emma. Tossed all night, dreams chasing me down for no good reason."

"I'm sorry to hear that." Emma kissed him on the cheek then passed him a cup and a plate of food. "I don't want you settling for leftovers. You need to keep up your strength. So sit down, say a blessing, and start eating."

Joseph had barely taken his place at the head of the table when the door burst open and the room filled with hungry soldiers. Emma placed the coffee pots on the table, a platter of fried pork, a large bowl of scrambled eggs, a pot of hot porridge and bread.

"You know I prefer my yolks soft on the top, daughter. Probably these men do too," Joseph said.

"I could stretch the portions better this way, Papa. Just eat it. I'll make them soft tomorrow." She'd added cow's milk to the beaten eggs, nearly doubling the amount in the bowl.

"It's just fine, Emma," James said. "We appreciate you feeding us again."

"Bread smells first rate, Miss Miller," said a young private who eagerly leaned in and grabbed a slice from the cutting board. She scampered over and slapped his fingers.

"If you recall, sir, this household prays before we partake." When Emma noted his forlorn face, she softened. "Perhaps you'd like to give thanks this morning, Mr...?"

"Charlie. You can call me Charlie," he said with a toothy grin and a body scan that caused her to squirm.

She ignored it and said, "Right, then let's pray."

When he finished his short talk with the Lord, the men dove into the food on the table. Within minutes the serving bowls were emptied and the ravenous lot chowed down everything in sight. She nodded politely at the many compliments that flew her way as she busied with the clean up. When she bent to pick up the water pail, James jumped to his feet.

"Let me help you, Emma."

"I'm fine, James. I need some fresh air, anyway." He did not accept no for an answer and followed Emma out the door. Remembering manners, she smiled but picked up the pace, not desiring a repeat of this morning's conversation.

"Did I mention you're looking real pretty today?"

She frowned on the inside but pasted a playful grin on her face. "Nice of you to say, but don't lie in hopes of sweet-talking me, James Fitzpatrick."

He rushed ahead to the well and grabbed the rope. "I'm not lying, Emma. I always loved your hair—the way the color lights up the blue in your eyes."

"You always loved to pull my pigtails and call me Red. And if I remember correctly, you claimed God made a huge mistake in creating a red-headed, blue-eyed, female creature to torment boys."

"Can't blame me for that. I was a young whipper-snapper back then," James argued. "But look; it's turned a softer shade now, almost like a pale strawberry. And I do love strawberries."

"Yes, you like bright, red strawberries and we both know it." Emma placed the empty pail at his feet. May as well let him feel like the gallant gentleman he fancied to portray this morning. "Personally, I believe color has nothing to do with your interest in my hair. You enjoy the tease." Emma noticed the wooden pail still hanging by the rope and nodded toward it. "Water, sir. The dishes won't wash without water."

James dropped the container into the well. She heard the splash as it hit the surface then watched him pull it back to the top, full to overflowing. Long strands of hair fell across his eyes; the man needed a haircut. If he had time to spare, she may have offered her services, but remained silent in fear of the line-up that would surely follow, for all his men appeared shabby and bedraggled. As he poured the clear cold liquid inside the house pail, his muscles bulged beneath his worn shirt; ones she didn't recall seeing when he left home as an eager young private. The war developed a man's strength in more ways than one. Some woman would appreciate the physical benefits brute force provided but cherish more the strength of character he'd gained as a leader.

He lifted the heavy load. "Looks like a promising morning, Emma. Sun's shedding some warmth our way; good day for riding."

"Where are you headed?" Emma asked.

"Colonel's setting up winter camp in New York. We're to meet up with the regiment there. Might be tempted to hang loose for a couple days if you'd walk to the lake and cast a line with me."

So much for his lack of free time.

"You've better things to do than go fishing with me." Before he could respond, she rambled on. "But thank you for coming all this way to bring Ethan home. Seemed fitting to have you say the words over him last night at his grave. You rekindled fond memories. My brother was a good man and didn't deserve to die so young." Emma attempted to hold back the bitterness.

"None do, Emma. Those Graybacks just keep fighting, even when it's clear they will lose," James said.

"As they should. God created all men equal. Surely he would not honor men that mistreat slaves and defile women for pleasure, then expect her to cook his family's meals." Emma's voice rose when she considered the injustice. "Riles me to no end imagining such ignorant men breathe the same air as we do."

"Yeah, well, like I said, they're taking a whooping. Shouldn't be too much longer," James said as they turned back toward the house. "Stay on guard, Emma. These are unsafe times in the country. St. Albans has escaped a lot of bloodshed, but there are traitors lurking in the woods wearing plain clothes and ready to spill their vile destruction on whoever gets in the way. Lots of cowards have high-tailed for Canada to wait out the fighting." He cleared his voice. "And you probably suspect by now that not all Union soldiers are gentlemen either."

She wondered if he referred to Charlie, the man seated at her table.

"There's good and bad in all people, James. I remind myself of that every night when I place the pistol on the night table next to me." She glanced toward the farmhouse. "I need to go inside. Your men will want clean plates to pack in their knapsacks."

Two hours later the small troop saddled up and prepared to head out. Although they represented a show of law, which helped to make her feel secure, Emma was grateful to see the last Union soldier disappear onto the main road. She stood on the porch and offered a brave smile, waving when James glanced back. She whispered a prayer that the Lord would keep him safe. With brotherly fondness, Emma hoped he would come to view her as a sister-figure, and not as a prospective wife. The thought brought clarity to his advances and Emma knew in her heart she could offer no more.

Later in the afternoon, she visited Ethan's grave. Emma sat on the cold earth beside the mound and with one finger outlined the cross that James had so thoughtfully placed as a marker. On the horizontal piece, he'd whittled, Ethan Miller—a brave soldier. That's not the picture Emma carried of him. If she could turn back the clock, she'd forget the last forty-two months ever happened and welcome the return of life prior to her world going crazy. But that was wishful thinking, and she'd do well to hold tight to reality. Nothing would ever be the same.

Not that she didn't believe in the cause. Her brothers had died to help free the Negroes, and that was a noble sacrifice. But victory came at a great cost to the Miller family. She could hear Ethan's laughter in the breeze, and it offered a measure of peace to her soul. Hugging his coat close, she smelled that horrid chewing tobacco he liked to roll around in his mouth until she wanted to smack him for flaunting the gross habit. Today, she'd gladly suffer the odor, for it stank of who he was, and she loved him dearly. Silent tears flowed. Emma rocked back and forth, whispering his name - but no one heard. In a second of time, the enemy had erased him from her life. Now he joined the ranks of thousands of deceased soldiers, some occupying nameless graves while the lucky corpses were returned to relatives for burial. Thanks to James, Ethan rested in his homeland.

After supper, Joseph pushed away from the table. "Good meal, Emma. You do your mother proud; God rest her soul."

"She taught me everything I know, so her influence will always fill this house, Papa. Encourages me to visualize her moving on to a better place, far from bloodshed, war, and sorrow."

"I should be with her." Joseph mumbled it, his tone executing strong conviction.

"Nonsense," Emma said. "Whatever would I do roaming around this big old farmhouse by myself?"

"That James Fitzpatrick comes from good stock. I think he hopes to set up housekeeping with you when he's finished killing the Rebs. You could live here and bring up a whole mess of young'uns for me to spoil."

"Papa, I'm not interested in settling here, or anywhere else with James. Mama always said *a woman knows in her heart when the right man comes along*. Why, James is like a brother to me."

Joseph remained silent behind her as she cleaned the after-dinner mess. Suddenly Emma heard him mutter in a faraway tone. "Don't be giving up on Ethan. He'll walk in that door soon. I can feel it in these old bones."

Emma whirled from the dishpan and stared at her father. Did she hear him right? He stood staring out the window, a strange expectation seeping through the lines in his face. She went to stand beside him. "Papa, you remember that Ethan came home with James, right? That we buried him beside Mama, and the markers we stuck in the ground for Mason and Henry?"

Joseph Miller's eyes glazed, and he patted her gently on the arm. "Keep the courage, daughter. I'm counting on you to help me hold the farm steady 'til we're all together as a family again."

Emma panicked. A make-believe account of the truth had replaced reality with the delusion that proved more to his liking. It invaded the forefront of his mind, and she wondered how deep inside he'd pushed the grave scene of yesterday. *Time will heal*— that's what Mama always said. He'd come around eventually. Losing three sons and a wife surely had the power to knock a sane man off his feet temporarily. The mind and heart could only handle so much pain. She stood on her tiptoes and kissed her father's cheek. "I love you, Papa. We'll hold the hill farm steady—you and me."

Chapter 3

TRIP TO TOWN

Two days later, Emma had collected enough eggs to bring to town. She debated on the blue or tan dress. These were her only choices left in the wardrobe, but she heard a faint ghostly whisper from her mother. *Wear the blue one, dear - it makes your eyes all soft, like a cool glass of water.* She smiled. It felt good to reminisce without the stabs of pain that usually accompanied her trips down memory lane. The garment hung loose in some spots because of the weight she'd lost, but in others filled out to accommodate her developing figure. The changes felt good. She forgot her resolve to throw away the work dress, and instead, figured she'd get the sewing basket out and spruce it up. It would be a long while before she could afford new material to rebuild her skimpy wardrobe.

Once positioned on a chair at the dressing table, Emma peered into the unforgiving mirror. She'd allowed her outer appearance to go downhill. Youthful features, which at her age should portray flawless and vibrant features, revealed only fatigue and discouragement. Her sea-blue eyes lacked the spark of life behind them, and her skin looked rubbery as the last signs of her summer tan disappeared behind the sun-cracked lines. The reflection in the mirror shocked her and produced a new resolve. Life should never boil down to placing one weary foot ahead of the other in an effort to make it through another monotonous day. Emma had allowed this horrid war to rule her disposition far too long. She wondered how many other women in the countryside had lost themselves in wartime shadows.

Pouring water into the basin, Emma soaked a washcloth with rose-fragrant soap and attempted to scrub the telltale signs away. But her effort merely resulted in a blood-pink rawness. Emma reached for her mother's jar of cream. Papa had purchased it for his wife and she'd been thrilled at the way it tickled her face, but Emma had not broken the seal once since her death, six months ago. Today, that false sense of loyalty ended. She lathered it on and worked it in, then closed her eyes to wait for the magic moment. It happened just as her mother had claimed, and she heard the faint whisper; *it feels good to be a woman, Emma. Never forget that.* She'd forgotten the whimsical way the woman's eyes twitched when she'd said those words. Now, standing at the door of womanhood, Emma concluded she best come to grips with the inevitable before some man planned her future for her.

Emma sighed. This musing proved unproductive, and she was no closer to leaving for town than she'd been a half-hour ago. She brushed her thick curls and knotted them at the back of her neck. From a round box, she removed her Sunday hat and held it in place on her head with a decorative pin her mother had given her two Christmases ago. Pinching her cheeks brought the natural glow to the surface, and she rubbed her lips again until they turned rosy. She stood and exhaled.

"This is as good as it gets, girl. It's time to face the world." She chuckled. Her neighbors had witnessed her tramping through mud-caked fields and also dressed in her finest Christmas dance attire – the worst and best of Emma Miller. Her feeble efforts today would fool no one.

The trip to St. Albans proved uneventful. She loved to saunter along the back road as if she were the only one left alive in the world. The squirrels appeared frantic to stash the last of the season's nuts and all of nature seemed to take a final breath of freedom anticipating the long winter's nap. The red, orange, and gold leaves of last week had dried up and with little strength left to hang on to the limb, fell from the trees under the command of the fall winds. It created a thick mat of color underfoot and as she stepped along, its crackle broke the silence.

When Emma rounded the corner and St. Albans came into view, she ground to an abrupt halt. She'd never seen so many people out and about this early in the morning. She picked up the pace and hurried, not wanting to miss any excitement.

The Statford Mercantile loomed in sight, and while her mind focused on the upcoming trade, Emma failed to notice the three men in the alleyway. They stepped out, barring her path. Surprised, she nearly dropped the basket of eggs, which made her angry and bolder than she should be with three rather domineering men surrounding her. The one touched her arm, and she bolted back.

"No need to be afraid, little miss. Just wanted to see if a real person lived under all that beauty." Emma instantly regretted her effort to appear at her best this morning. She'd attracted the wrong sort before even encountering one familiar face.

Emma regained her self-control when she noticed the leering expressions. "Excuse me, gentlemen. I have business in town."

"Business? My, they make 'em pretty here in Vermont, don't they, Smiley? What kinds of business are you headed to?"

"The mercantile, although I fail to see where that is any of your concern, sir." The speaker did not appear to receive rejection well from a woman for his face reddened with embarrassment as he glanced at his friends to gauge their response. They spurred him on.

"No need to get huffy," he said, trying to sound respectable while peeking under the checked cloth napkin that covered the eggs. "Well, lookie here; fresh laid today, boys. Maybe we can skip that trip to the diner. Got us all the breakfast we need right here and a woman to cook it."

Emma pushed the basket closer to her side. As a result, one egg rolled from the top layer and fell onto the boarded walkway, the shell breaking and forming a yellow blob of precious commodity. She squealed with dismay, but that only triggered more taunting from the men encircling her. Another hand reached out, caressing her neck, and she gasped with repulsion.

"Now we can do this your way or the fun way. Which will it be, little woman?"

A new voice from behind cut through, causing the men to divide, as if trained to jump when an officer barked. A random thought hit her—could these men visiting St. Albans possibly be Confederates? In the furthermost part of Vermont, not much violence had occurred, but random rounds of looting from stragglers coming over from New York or down from Canada. The men accosting her did not wear uniforms, but that was not unusual. The sad fact was that most times common folks couldn't tell from appearance what side a soldier fought on. Even accents couldn't identify them as Union or Confederate soldiers, as the Border States had men enlisted with both sides of the war. But they possessed an army attitude, and their presence suddenly filled her with a new sense of dread. James had warned her to be wary, and she'd walked smack-dab into a hornet's nest.

"Let the lady pass, boys. No need for carousing this early in the morning."

Emma noticed a tall man dressed in gray pants and a green shirt leaning against the wall. He removed his hat and smiled openly at Emma. "Good morning, miss. May I escort you to your destination?"

The three rogues reluctantly backed away, and Emma breathed a sigh of relief. Although she had no desire to keep company with this new man, she preferred his kind eyes to the taunting of the others.

"Thank you, sir. It's not far. I'm bringing eggs and cheese to sell at the store."

He reached for Emma's arm, and with no options available, she took hold of it. His smile was genuine and displayed a friendliness that did not threaten her independence. Nor did it appear marred with hatred and anger, as was the case with the mischief-makers a moment ago. Not even defeat and discouragement saddened his eyes, and she felt suddenly refreshed just to gaze upon him. His countenance provided hope and validation for her morning's resolution.

"The name is William Davis, ma'am, at your service."

"And am I to feel safer with a smooth talker such as yourself, Mr. Davis?"

He laughed heartily and unpretentiously. "I see your point. But yes, you can feel safer." He glanced at her basket. "Although eggs and cheese are a great temptation for a hungry man these days."

"Those men were not hungry for eggs and cheese, sir. The lot of them disgust me."

"You don't live in town?"

She grinned. "And you think it wise of me to reveal that information to a stranger?"

"Perhaps one who rescued you?"

"You are a silver-tongued man. I shall be wary of you as well."

"You are a wise woman." He stopped, and it surprised her they'd arrived at the mercantile. "Delivered safely to your destination. Have a good day." He tipped his hat and she could not stop her heart from skipping a beat when he beamed with unabashed admiration.

"Thank you for your kindness, sir." Emma's voice held a slight tremor that embarrassed her, and she pivoted and disappeared behind the store door and shut it firmly.

Emma inhaled deeply before she walked to the counter. Only one female customer searched through the bolts of cloth and the owner of the mercantile stood behind the counter writing in his ledger. When he noticed her, his face brightened.

"Emma, so glad to see you. We heard about your brother Ethan. You've experienced far too much loss out at the hill farm. The wife and me are praying for you and your father."

"Thank you, Mr. Statford. We appreciate it."

"What have you for me today?" Emma passed him the basket and cast a sideways glance at the material. Brilliant fall colors and patterns wooed her, and she marveled at this new longing. Vanity was a new experience and she inwardly questioned if she should talk to the man of God about this worldly compulsion.

"Emma," said Mr. Statford. "Do you want me to credit your account or do you have a purchase today?"

She turned from the temptation.

"I need a tin of coffee. Used a lot yesterday when the Union soldiers showed up unexpectedly."

He reached on the shelf behind him and placed her purchase under the cover in the basket on the counter. "You be careful walking home. A couple new rowdy fellas showed up here last night to join the others. Place is crawling with disorderly strangers who like to stay up late. Hardly got a wink of sleep with all the commotion."

"Is that so, Mr. Statford?" came a slick voice from behind. "That wasn't our intention. Just out for a bit of fun. Fact is, a bunch of friends are arriving in St. Albans over the next while; meeting up to plan a sporting event and enjoy some entertainment if that's all right? Nice town you got here."

"We like it." Mr. Statford never batted an eye. "What can I help you with this morning?"

"Now that's right friendly." A young man in his early twenties, Emma would guess, crossed the room in four easy strides and reached for Charles Statford's hand, shaking it long and hard. "Name's Bennett Yonge and pleased to make your acquaintance."

The visitor had an aura of confidence that filled the room. He wore a new set of clothes and a black felt hat, which he removed when he noticed Emma. "Pardon, miss. Were you finished?"

"Yes. Have a good day, sir," Emma said, picking up her basket.

"Don't rush off. A couple boys and me are staying at the Tremont Hotel. Would you care to join us for lunch?"

"I couldn't. I have a full day planned."

The stranger shrugged and turned toward Statford. "I have a list here." He withdrew a folded paper from his pocket and passed it to the storekeeper. "Won't need it until the eighteenth when I leave for home, but wanted to get it in early—not knowing how well you kept your store supplied." His accent captivated Emma and she lingered a few steps behind. He tossed a coin on the counter. "Let the pretty lady pick out some ribbon for her hair—it's on me." Bennett tipped his hat in Emma's direction and grinned.

"That's unnecessary," Emma said and moved toward the door to exit. On second thought, she stopped, unprepared to leave the safety of the building. She wandered to the back of the store and pretended to appear interested at the items on a shelf. She listened to the interaction from a distance and gasped when Bennett suddenly appeared in front of her, bowed and passed her a whole sleeve of yellow ribbon. He winked and left without another word.

Emma hurried to the counter where Mr. Statford was mopping the sweat from his brow.

"Not sure what made me nervous about the man. Seems pleasant enough, but something's smoldering on the inside; like smoke ready to burst into flame."

"I know what you mean," Emma said.

"Some are right nice and others, not so friendly," Mr. Statford said.

"I think I met the latter group outside." Emma placed the yellow ribbon on the counter. "You keep this—what would I do with all this yellow ribbon?"

"He paid for it. Might look nice woven through a new dress. You should treat yourself."

"Maybe when the war is over." Emma glanced out the window. "But it is sad to see our peaceful hometown invaded by ruffians and bullies. Perhaps you should try the tactics I use at home and hide a good bit of your inventory. You can dig it out for regulars, but it may stop others from cleaning you out should they become greedy and decide not to pay for purchases."

"That's a good idea, Emma." He held up the bolt. "Last chance. He left money for this, Emma. Are you sure you don't want it—for later?"

"Sure she does." Emma whirled around to face George Conger, James's uncle, and retired war hero from the first Vermont Calvary.

"Oh, hello, Mr. Conger," Emma said. "Did

you see James when he was here?"

"Nope, the boy is too busy to come calling. War takes all a man's time and focus." He hit his leg. "This is what happens when you take your eyes off the enemy."

"Yes, even while suffering the pain you saved many that day," Mr. Statford said.

The man looked embarrassed. "Now, if you're finished in town, Miss Miller, I will escort you home. James would appreciate me doing that for his girl."

Emma raised her eyebrows and started to contradict James's claim on her but then decided against it. It would all sort out in the end.

"Thank you, Mr. Conger, but I'm sure that's uncalled for."

"Too many scallywags have noticed you wander in this morning. I'd recommend you not return to town until it's safe."

"But what about my trading? It's the bigger source of our income these days?" Emma said.

"I'll try to stop out sometime and bring whatever you have to town. Mr. Statford can credit your account 'til you get back to do your own shopping."

Emma looked at the storekeeper and he nodded. "Sounds like a good idea, Emma."

She begged to differ. It was not her nature to back down from bullies, but when she saw James' concern mirrored in George's face, she gave in.

"Fine. Since they are pulling out on the eighteenth, I suppose I can sit tight and wait it out."

"Thank goodness they won't be here for Butter Day," Mr. Statford said.

"Oh, yes, that would be dreadful. Good day, Mr. Statford." Emma reached for the arm George offered and with the basket in hand left and headed home.

Chapter 4

THE NIGHT VISITOR

They hadn't walked ten feet when James slipped in quietly beside them. "Oh, James, what are you doing here?" Emma asked.

"Went by the farm and Joseph told me you'd come to town. Followed—just to make sure you were all right."

"James, I told you I'd be fine. And look, your uncle stepped in to escort me home."

James nodded at the man who still limped from his injury. "Thanks, Uncle, but I can take it from here. It's quite a stretch to the farm and the lady and me have a fishing date. I'm visiting on borrowed time."

It was on the tip of Emma's lips to tell him her day's plans had not included him but when she looked at his eager face, she surrendered. Her father might enjoy a plate of fish for supper. Of late she'd avoided the wooded areas, so she rarely went to her favorite fishing hole in Lake Champlain.

They visited for a few minutes with George then moved toward the dirt road that led home. Emma groped for a conversation starter.

"There are several men who've settled into the hotels to plan some sporting event. Do you know anything about it?"

"They told me at the depot some traveled as far as Burlington and Essex Junction and then doubled back north, either by train or carriage, to St. Albans. Some others came straight in from Canada."

"Do you suppose they didn't want people to know straight off that they gathered as a group?" Emma asked.

"Possible, but it seems redundant. The town is pleased as punch to take money for the activities and pleasures those men enjoy."

"Are they all staying together?"

"No, the bunch is spread out like a herd of wandering sheep. Some are housed at the American Hotel at the corner of North Main and Lake Streets, and others laid up at the St. Albans House at the corner of Lake and Catherine Streets. A few are rooming at Willard's Boarding House on Lake Street. Seem to have strategic points all around town."

"Does that worry you, James? Should you not send a wire to the general?"

"Already did, but he's more interested in the skirmish happening in New York. The country is too big for the army to cover effectively. Senseless scattering small groups of soldiers every time a rumor hits the air."

Emma nodded, for there was strength in numbers. Strategically a show of great force in one location to do battle would eventually win the war. "I understand."

"I think the gents are who they say; a bunch of sports enthusiasts meeting up. It'll do folks good to see physical activity on the sports field rather than the kind played out on the frontline." James studied Emma and continued. "Although I haven't talked to one directly—like you." Emma saw a fleck of jealousy cross his face. He'd been stalking her. "Saw you walking with one of them earlier—arm in arm. You need to be more careful."

"If you saw that, then why was he the one to come to my rescue when those horrible men cornered me?"

"I missed that part," he blurted. "Did they hurt you?"

"No! Thanks to the man who escorted me to the mercantile and delivered me safely inside."

"He looks like a traitor, even if he's wearing street clothes."

"Perhaps, but a kind one, apparently. I'll not judge him by which side of this cursed battle he's chosen to fight on. Every man has his own story."

"That doesn't sound patriotic, Emma. What about our cause?"

"Phooey! I'm tired of it all, James Fitzpatrick and just want those still alive to make it home, wherever that may be. You said yourself the war is tipping in our favor. The slaves will be free, and that's all that really matters."

"I can see you're tired. Perhaps fishing is not a good idea today."

"Perhaps you're right." The idea of a fish supper flew by the wayside, and in her mind she settled for the leftover roast beef that awaited her father's pleasure.

She felt bad for his sake that his idea had backfired, but at the same time relieved that she'd not find herself trapped in a conversation about her future which he presumed included him. Sometimes she didn't care for the rigid army man that James had become, but supposed it might be necessary for a captain in the army. He strolled next to her, holding the reins of his horse plodding along behind them. Feeling his moodiness, she steered clear of any topic that might unsettle him more, which was pretty much life at the moment. Silence was the better option.

When they reached the bottom step of the porch, she acknowledged him and offered the biggest smile she could muster. "Thank you for your help today, James. You are a good friend. Please, take care of yourself."

He caught Emma totally off guard when he leaned over and planted a quick kiss on her cheek.

"Thinking about you and our future together will keep me going. Goodbye, Emma." He jumped on his horse and sped out the laneway before the kiss or his words registered fully in her mind.

Her father was inside and pounced on her the moment she opened the door. "Letting a man kiss you? Where's your decency, daughter?"

Emma did not need this reprimand. She barked back. "He stole it, the same way two strangers in town thought they could steal my innocence."

"What?"

"Swarms of men claiming to be a sporting group, have invaded St. Albans. I suspect they could be Rebs but at the moment, are conducting themselves mannerly, for the most part. Probably the town merchants will profit from the extra business."

"Good Lord, Emma. You say they accosted you right in our hometown?"

"Yes, but thankfully, there are still gentlemen to defend a lady's honor. The first was a kind stranger, and the other George Conger, until James appeared to walk me home." Emma noticed the anger marring her father's face and matched it with her own. "So, Joseph Miller, if you presume that me allowing a poor soldier returning to battle for the cause a quick kiss on my cheek to be immoral behavior, then I fear you must reconsider your convictions." She hoped that would settle his mood.

"I should go to town," Joseph said.

"You should not! James advised us to sit tight."

Joseph grumbled, "Should have gone to war myself. Would have been easier to die than sit here and watch others do it for me."

"You'd be useless to the Union, Papa. That bum leg lets you work at your own pace around here, but it would surely have given out running for your life. So, we will not hear another word about that nonsense."

"You sound like your mother."

"Of course I do. Us Miller women knew how to tackle the likes of the males who work our farmstead—worked, I suppose is more accurate now."

"You missed lunch. I just nibbled on some pork grinds and dipped my bread in the sweet syrup."

"Oh, Papa. That's not good for you. Sugar makes your head go fuzzy. Are you feeling all right?"

"Feeling dandy. You need not coddle me, daughter."

"That is a matter of opinion. I'll start supper soon, and we'll eat early. Got some beef roast left to serve up."

Later that evening, when Emma tired of listening to her father snore on the big comfy chair next to the fireplace, she shooed him off to bed. It was still too early to retire, so she puttered around the downstairs with a cleaning cloth and a broom. Satisfied with the results, she went to the cookstove for a well-deserved cup of tea. She glanced at the woodbox and groaned. Her father hadn't filled it and she hated not having enough in the morning. Plenty enough chores without worrying about fuel for the stove.

Emma threw a jacket over her dress and hurried outside, dusk not the ideal time of day to be roaming the premises. On her third trip to the pile, she saw movement. It caught her by surprise but she recovered quickly, hoping she'd not given herself away. She scolded herself for the nervousness that festered inside. Her first assumption should have conjured up images of animals prowling around the yard, not two-legged intruders. But caution dictated the rules she lived by now, so after the third trip to the woodpile, she called it quits. She pulled the board across the casing of the back door and locked herself in the farmhouse.

In the sitting room she found her father's gun, which lately he forgot to bring upstairs at night. She checked, and inside the chamber was one bullet. Should she run for hers? A noise startled her, and she ran to the window. The shadow of a man hunched in the near darkness sprang her into action. Suddenly she remembered that she'd not locked the front door. Emma raced toward it and arrived in time to hear the thump of boots coming up the outside steps—his plan obviously not a sneak approach. A loud noise shattered against the door and she dashed to a nearby window to see the staggering figure struggle to remain on his feet. What if it were a Union soldier? It was her duty to open the door and nurse his wounds. She strained her eyes for some form of recognition, and then it hit her.

The gentleman who'd come to her rescue this morning waited outside. Whatever was he doing prowling around the farm this time of night? She supposed none of the details mattered. He'd saved her from harm and she owed him. But had he followed her here? Was he a quiet stalker as opposed to the rowdy more forward bunch he'd disciplined earlier? Indecision paralyzed her. The man could be dying, and she stood debating her personal safety. Hurrying forward, she cautiously opened the door, her gun aimed ready to defend herself. The man collapsed into her arms and they landed on the floor in a heap.

The odor of fresh bath soap penetrated her senses, followed by light-headedness secreting from the crack she'd received by the butt of his rifle in the tumble. Emma squeezed out from under the weight of his body, bounded to the door, and peered into the silent night. Convinced he'd come alone, she slammed it shut and bolted it securely. Her brain refused to focus on the fact that she'd just locked herself inside with a possible Confederate soldier. No time to split hairs. The man was one of God's creatures, and she'd do no less for an injured animal, let alone one who'd gallantly stood against his own to protect her this morning.

Dropping to the floor, she stretched him flat. The smiling countenance that had captivated Emma earlier now seemed strained and the lines on his face etched with pain. Blood oozed from under his shirt. With shaking fingers, Emma unbuttoned it, all the while biting her lip at such brazen conduct while alone with a stranger.

She pushed away the awkwardness, surely by now accustomed to seeing a bare-chested man. For since the outbreak of the war, the Union had dropped nine wounded soldiers on her doorstep to nurse back to health.

At sixteen, she'd worked with the town doctor during an epidemic, and since then the locals imagined she also possessed the gift of healing and brought their sick to her instead of going to town. Emma discouraged such practice, but backwoods folks held fast to strange, old-fashioned ways and continued to drop by. But this man lying on her floor was not local, and she feared neighbors would not understand or approve of her housing a traitor to the flag, even an injured one. If James were present, he'd probably finish him off, and send his sorry soul to hell. Whereas, Emma did not believe God somehow preferred northerners to those raised in the south. All men created in His image possessed a soul and an equal opportunity for the gift of redemption—no matter how misguided their minds concerning the slavery of black families for personal gain.

Mentally, Emma resumed the debate while she laid open his shirt. It was her Christian duty to take care of strangers in need; the Bible suggested the possibility of entertaining angels. She chuckled at that stretch of the Holy Scriptures, for she could credit nothing virtuous within her raging emotions that might warrant such a noble visitation. She forced her mind to concentrate on the task at hand. The curly, blond chest hairs were stained red, and she saw the source of the injury. A bullet. Lifting his shoulders, she noticed that it was a clean shot, not hitting anything vital. His body trembled.

He stirred, and through glazed eyes attempted a smile. "We meet again."

"You're shot. I need to get you into the back room. Can you stand?"

He nodded and attempted to shuffle his body. "First bullet in over three years."

"Consider yourself one of the lucky ones, sir." She attempted to hide the regret that while this man received only one bullet, deadly bullets on battlefields had snuffed the life from her brothers, erasing them from the face of the earth. "This one is not fatal."

"Pleased to hear that."

She pushed to her knees and wrapped an arm around his good shoulder. "Please, sir. You cannot remain lying in my entranceway. It's dangerous for all of us."

Emma watched him recoil. "I'm sorry. Never considered the position this would put you in. Help me to the door and I'll leave."

"And bleed to death? You'll do nothing of the kind. Besides, the temperature is dropping tonight and you're in shock."

"I am mighty cold." His tortured eyes debated his options. "Maybe just for tonight."

"Agreed," she said. "Now help me get you tucked into the warm cot next to a potbelly stove so I can tend to your wound."

Her father had set up the small room behind the kitchen for her to nurse any who came calling. She stored medical supplies there, some the doctor had provided but mostly natural herbs she found in the woods. He appreciated the help, for his practice covered a huge area and his travels often left the infirmary empty of immediate help.

William Davis grunted aloud as they stretched him flat on the cot. Emma pulled at his boots and he put up his hands for her to stop. "A man sleeps in his boots these days." When Emma raised her eyebrows in disbelief, he continued, "Haven't taken them off for a long time, except to wash my feet and change my socks. Soldier needs to be ready to move out at any given moment."

"So, you admit you are a soldier—in the Confederate army?" Emma prodded.

He cussed under his breath. "Figured you'd guessed by now, listening to all the foreign accents of the men in town."

"I suspected as much."

"Does that change your mind about tending to my wound?"

"You are one of God's creatures. I will take out the bullet, sir, and you can leave your boots on, even though it will provide extra work cleaning your dirty sheets tomorrow."

As Emma rummaged through baskets of supplies, William said, "Appears I came to the right house. Are you a nurse?"

"No, but I help the doctor out now and then. Besides, many women have had to learn some basic nursing to bandage soldiers who bang on their doors in the night." Emma raised her eyebrows. "What were you doing here, in my woods, at this late hour?"

He guarded his expression. "Watching, in case your admirers paid a visit."

"Did everyone follow me home from town?" Emma's voice sounded brave, but she hid her eyes from his scrutiny.

"Only one, but he won't be following you any more, Miss Miller."

Emma spun around. "If that's true, it appears I am twice indebted to you." She offered a smile and watched as his lit up his green eyes. This man could play havoc with a woman's heart. "How do you know my name?"

"Did some nosing around. Sorry if that offends you, but our brief encounter in town left quite an impression on me." He groaned, and she hurried over with a tray of supplies.

"I need to wash these tools," she said. I don't want infection to set in. I'll bring in some of my Pa's brandy—for the pain."

He grabbed her arm stopping her departure and studied her close. When she began to squirm under his watchful eye, he said, "Thank you."

"You're welcome, Mr. Davis. I'll be right back. Close your eyes and rest."

Chapter 5

HOUSING THE ENEMY

The minor surgery went well, and William proved an excellent patient, gritting his teeth and persevering the constant digging inside the injured area. The bullet lodged close to the entrance point on his upper shoulder, and its removal proved an easier task than some she'd done. She soaked the bandage with a healing paste and plastered it in place. He endured the procedure bravely while swimming in a pool of sweat, but close to the end, the patient fell unconscious. Emma was grateful. The contrast of pain and valor continuously altered his expression and caused a noticeable distraction for the young woman. The man held a startling resemblance to her brother Ethan, and that intimacy bound her to the stranger with an uncomfortable awareness. Shaking herself free of the spell, Emma bathed his face with a cool cloth then covered his body with the blanket.

In the kitchen, she cleaned her tools and set a soup broth to simmer for the night. When she returned, she wiped his fevered face, noting the refined character oozing from his being. This man was unaccustomed to hard work—perhaps one of those arrogant men from the south that she so loathed. The odd twitch caused his body to spasm violently, and the nightmares screwed his face into unrecognizable twists. She knew he'd endured as much as any man fighting the good fight and chided herself for being judgmental.

Before she settled to watch her patient for the night, Emma brought her father's pistol with the one shell inside and William Davis's rifle into the back room. She stoked all the wood stoves then pulled the rocker close to her patient's cot. Wrapping a quilt around her shoulders, she settled in for a long night.

Emma wakened often throughout her watch, checking his bandage and mopping his brow, but mostly mesmerized by his ragged breathing that expanded his muscular chest then let it collapse in exhaustion. An odd groan escaped his lips, whether it originated from dreams or pain she couldn't tell. She'd used her small supply of willow-bark sparingly. There would be others to lie on this cot, those with greater pain requiring relief. Her mind refused to debate if his Confederate status weighed in on that decision. The war had diminished the simplest, most common response to human need to the question of what side a man fought for. Being confronted with that awful possibility brought shame to her soul.

In the wee hours of the morning she heard him cough. She stirred and bounced to her feet.

"Good morning, Mr. Davis. How are you feeling?"

"I believe it was the best sleep I've had in a long time."

"The alcohol might have something to do with that," Emma said.

"Or the fact that I feel safe with a woman guarding me with a gun on her lap." William grinned, and she saw a mischievous twinkle in his eye. He'd uncovered her dual purpose in keeping the firearm close at hand – to protect her patient against anyone attempting to kill him, or herself against the man who lay on the cot.

Emma enjoyed a sense of humor. "Glad to hear my presence made you feel secure. Let me check your wound."

Shifting closer, Emma felt his eyes study her every move. The crimson flush had lessened. "You still have a fever, but not nearly as bad as last night. I believe you are on the mend." She picked up the basin. "We'll continue the cool wipes. I have broth on the stove, not your ideal breakfast, but in your case, better for now. I'll be right back."

She hurried into the kitchen for cool water. The pail was empty, and Emma murmured under her breath. Abandoning all good sense, she raced coatless to the well and filled the tin pail. Back inside, she half-filled the basin and returned to the sickroom to find her father standing at the bottom of the cot. A shocked expression filled William's face while Joseph Miller sounded jubilant.

Joseph noticed his daughter and directed his chatter her way. "Look here, Emma! God answered prayer, and my birthday candle wish, all in one sweep. Ethan's come home."

"Papa?" Emma could hardly believe her ears. True, William possessed a likeness to Ethan, but not one that would fool a father.

Joseph noticed her with the basin of water. "Good thinking, girl. He's got a fever. Bring it over and let's douse his forehead. We must move him upstairs, just in case those Rebs from town make their way out to the farm."

"Move him upstairs?" Emma showed confusion as she tried to wrap her head around the conversation.

"Emma, don't stand there with your mouth hanging open. Wipe the boy down, then we'll get him to his room."

"Ethan's room?" Dumbfounded she glanced at William who appeared as bewildered as she, though he had the good sense to stay out of the conversation.

Joseph grabbed the basin. "Land sakes, Emma. Go pull the sheets back and air the room out. I'll bring him up myself after I soak up his sweat."

Emma cast pleading eyes toward the patient and bit her bottom lip. He seemed to read the situation better than she had and smiled. "It's okay, Emma. Do as he says." She backed out of the room and collapsed against the kitchen wall. Dear God, Papa was not in his right mind. She inched away from the wall and regained strength to head upstairs.

Emma opened the door to her brother's bedroom. She'd not gone inside for many months. It smelled stuffy and its vacancy possessed a chill of death—Ethan's death. How could she allow this charade to continue? She remembered her plan to show her father the gravesite today and shuddered at the folly of that trip now that he imagined his son to be home and merely injured.

Hurrying to the window she yanked open the striped curtains and lifted the pane to allow fresh air inside. At the bed, she inhaled, barely able to complete the task, and gingerly pulled back the top blankets. The white sheets were clean and unused, that fact alone causing another piece of her heart to dry up. With a sweeping motion, she brushed the sheets slow and lovingly and observed a tear drop onto the surface. And another. Emma wiped them away. Enough with the sentiments. All her emotions could cope with at this point was tending to the living.

While gripping the top blankets, she hung them out the open window shaking them the best she could, then remade the bed. Noticing a towel by the washbasin, she used it to dust the frame of the bed and the night tables, skimming off an eighth-inch of hard dust.

The sounds of dragging feet and puffing men reached her ears, and she raced for the door.

Emma moved to the other side of William, relieving her father of carrying the majority of weight. "You're almost there." She could feel the heat radiating from his body. She glanced at her father and he read the concern in her expression.

"Don't fret. Think it's just the body warding off infection. The skin around his wound is red, but not dark and sickly."

Emma nodded. "We'll watch it close, Papa."

Again, William offered nothing to the conversation. The move upstairs had done him in. The trio made it to the bed and this time William Davis did not argue when Joseph pulled off his boots and placed them close beside the night table.

Joseph sat on a chair next to the bed and spoke. "I got this, daughter. We need nourishment. Some broth for our boy here, and I'm near starved exerting all this energy before breakfast."

Emma smiled. Some things never changed. "I'll leave you to it then."

Downstairs, she stirred the fire and began to prepare breakfast. Outside the sound of a horse drew her attention. She rushed to the window and peered out. It was James. He'd said he was pulling out yesterday. Emma groaned. If her father noticed, he'd be down in a flash hailing the good news of his son's return home. Then James would know she'd nursed the enemy and no good would come of that for any of them.

Chapter 6

MISTAKEN IDENTITY

Using her hands, Emma ironed the wrinkles out of her dress and tucked a few loose strands of hair behind her ears. At the door she pulled back the board and opened it wide to welcome the early morning visitor.

"James! What a pleasant surprise," Emma said. Mustering a cheerful greeting proved harder than expected when her voice cracked under the tension. She repeated her question. "I thought you'd left for New York?"

"My conscience wouldn't let me go without apologizing for my forward behavior and badgering you with my plans for us." Genuine concern flowed from James, causing Emma additional guilt.

Recalling his claim that hopes of a future with her kept him alive, she bit her tongue. Would the right time to set him straight ever present itself? "No apology is necessary, James. I'm not going anywhere and the war rages on. You need to stay focused."

James regarded her closely. "Are you coming down with a cold? Ma always said this was the worst time of year. No one dressed warm enough for outside and refused to accept that the long winter lurked around the corner."

Emma cleared her throat. She'd need to calm down and appear natural, for James's discernment was on full alert. "Oh, no, I'm fine. Just off to a late start today, scurrying around to put a meal on the table. Can I fix you something before you leave?" She bit her lower lip. He'd not even crossed the threshold, and she was pushing him away. Reaching for his arm, she pulled him inside, out of view from the upstairs window, should Joseph be watching.

"Kind of you to offer. Can't stay long. Just needed to clear the air. The company is moving slowly, so I'll catch up before nightfall."

"Papa is not up yet, so I'll feed you first and have you on your way before he even shows his face downstairs." Emma hoped.

James glanced toward the stairwell. "Thought he'd be out on the land by now?"

"He's under the weather. Ethan's death has been hard to accept – him being the last son." Emma smiled to hide her fear, for James could not understand the emotional dump the news had wreaked on her father; but she'd not speak of it today.

As Emma grabbed a fry pan and two of yesterday's eggs, James said, "Don't fuss, Emma. Just some homemade bread and your strawberry jam will be fine."

"I can have eggs whipped up before you drink your first cup of coffee, James Fitzpatrick." She nodded to the pot she'd set to brew on the stove. "Help yourself." As he filled his cup, she cracked the eggs in the pan and covered them. From the counter she brought slices of bread and grabbed the jar of preserves. Placing a fork, knife, and spoon in front of James, she smiled.

"So, I gather with your leaving the area, there's no action close by? That's a relief," Emma said and blushed, realizing her concern was for the man upstairs.

"Other than the newcomers in St. Albans, it seems to be quiet in these parts. Might face trouble west of here. One last plug before we set up camp for winter."

A flood of relief swept over Emma. William Davis could heal properly and depart her home in peace to join his friends, plan their event, and leave the territory. It scared her to realize how much that time frame pleased her. But accepting that no one would discover him sprawled in Ethan's bed while attempting to appease her father's delusions eased her growing concerns.

She flipped the soft-yoked eggs onto a plate and placed it in front of James. "Just the way you like them."

"We know so much about one another, Emma. Seems only right we get together after this war plays out." He bit off the crust of his bread and talked with his mouth full. "Now I know I said I'd not badger you, but you must know a man needs encouragement."

Emma groaned inwardly. This was not a subject she wanted to pursue this morning. "After the war, we'll have plenty of time to explore that possibility. Perhaps moving forward we'll find our goals changed."

"I know what I want. Work the land like our fathers did before us."

Emma busied herself at the counter and began to hum a tune to calm her spirit. "Suppose I won't be attending church Sunday since you don't want me walking to town."

"Good idea to stay fixed at the farm." James pushed to his feet. "Sorry to eat and run but I need to shove off. Boys want to stop at the Gander Saloon before we hit the border—have a bit of fun before engaging in another battle."

Emma turned and tried not to show the relief in her face. She picked up a loaf of bread. "Well, you take this along and share it."

"Thank you, Emma. You have a kind heart."

"As do you." She took his arm and headed to the door. "Time for me to shake Papa awake. The day is not waiting on any of us."

"Give him my regards." James took the porch steps two at a time and mounted his horse, offering a quick wave to Emma as he turned up the winding laneway. At least he'd spared her the goodbye kiss this time.

Hurrying inside, she began to prepare a tray for William. Whatever had they been doing the entire time James sat in the kitchen? She scooped broth into a bowl for the patient along with a cup of weak tea. For her, one thick slice of buttered bread and a mug of coffee made it on the tray to bring upstairs. On the table she set a bowl of porridge, a pitcher of milk, soft eggs, a thin slab of ham, two slices of bread, butter and jam for her father, in hopes he'd come down to eat and give her a chance to talk with the patient alone.

Emma mounted the steps and exhaled deeply before entering Ethan's bedroom. Joseph sat staring at the figure on the bed while William pretended to be asleep. His eyes darted open when Emma entered.

Joseph sprang to his feet. "Heard the rider, but noticed it was only James. Knew you'd be fine without our help." He chuckled as he gazed with admiration at the man in the bed. "I stayed out of sight, not wanting the Union soldiers to be stealing back my boy so soon. He's not healed yet and I'm not done visiting."

William's eyes pleaded with Emma to help. She'd left him in an awkward situation. "Papa, take a break. I've set your breakfast out on the kitchen table. I'll feed…" she almost said Ethan, but decided not to feed his confusion, "our patient. You could use the time to plan your day."

"Suppose chores need doing," Joseph muttered as he moved toward the door. "And there's fences to mend." He shook his head and looked back to find two sets of eyes staring at his departure. "Sorry, lad. Winter will be here before we know it."

William spoke. "Don't worry about me. Emma will have me doing cartwheels in no time."

Joseph brightened. "Good. I could use your opinion about the north field."

Emma interrupted. "You go on now, Papa, before your breakfast gets cold. I'll serve lunch up here in the room so you can visit again." It was good to see his smile, and she secretly wished the lie could continue forever.

A voice intruded her thoughts. "What are you smiling about? We have an uncomfortable situation before us."

Emma turned to William. "Agreed. But it is a relief to see my father happy again. His behavior lately is disconcerting."

"You don't need to tell me that. He looks straight at me and calls me Ethan, who I gather from his rambling is your brother."

"My dead brother. We buried him earlier in the week in the family plot."

William whistled. "This must be difficult for you. I tried to play along until you got back to set things right. Meanwhile, I've been racking my brains for an excuse to leave—like we agreed last night. I figure if I leave before he returns, you can tell him how loyal to the Union I am and that I needed to get to camp before they pulled out." He raised his eyebrows. "They are pulling out of the area soon, right?"

Emma picked up a cloth napkin and threw it across his chest. "You expect me to snitch on the Union army?" She grabbed his good arm. "Scooch up in the bed so you don't make a mess."

"Sorry, that was not my intention in asking." A few moans later, he sat repositioned. Emma took the seat that her father had occupied next to the bed and dipped the spoon into the bowl.

"Open wide, Mr. Davis." Emma brought the spoon toward his mouth and he accepted it with a weak smile.

Emma noticed his eyes misting and wondered in which direction his mind ventured as he gazed beyond her into a world he'd left behind.

"Have you lost family in the war?" Emma asked.

"One brother that I know of. I joined a regiment far from my homeland." Between bites, he added, "My company moved north right from the start. Thought it might be easier."

"Easier?" she asked. "A life in the north is just as precious as one from the south. Why so picky?"

"You want the honest answer or one drilled into us?"

"Always honesty."

"Well, Miss Miller, I like to think of myself as a man with deep convictions worthy of defending with a sword. But this war is not one of them." When Emma appeared surprised, he continued, "My family is true southerners—plantation and slaves included—the whole lifestyle that both sides are fighting for and against. And solidarity, according to my father, was compulsory. He demanded that the *Davis* clan show a unified front to support the family cause. The entire litter of six boys swore allegiance to the Confederate flag, and when I, the seventh and youngest hesitated, my father set me straight as to whom I owed my loyalty."

"Are you implying you might have joined the Union had it not been for family pressure?" Emma asked.

"Kentucky is a border state and I might add supporting the Union army to help bring this war to a close. I considered switching more than once, but couldn't stomach the possibility that I might someday end up battling my kin. That nightmare alone keeps me Confederate to the end."

His eyes darkened, revealing all was not as it seemed. A mystery shadowed him and it kindled her curiosity, but not to the point of prying. It was neither her business nor right to siphon secrets from the man.

Emma forced another spoonful into his mouth. "One more to help build your strength. Your family will need your modern thinking when the North wins this war and gentlemen from the South are forced into manual work. That, or pay for hired help."

"Not an easy transition, especially for my father's generation who have flourished behind the travesty. With wealth comes power, and such a man will not bow easily when it involves losing control over slaves."

Emma faltered for words. In her entire life, she'd never suspected meeting a Southern-raised man who talked of humanity in this manner.

"You have your mouth open, Miss Miller." Emma clamped it shut. "Why is that a hint of prejudice I see in your face, my sweet Northern lady?"

Prejudice. Could it be true? Raised in Vermont, she had her own slant on truth and never once considered that others, predisposed to different sources of influence, felt equally justified in their thinking. "I am ashamed to say yes. You are a surprise to me, William Davis."

"A pleasant one I hope."

Emma blushed and rose to her feet. Laying a hand on his forehead, she said, "Your fever is almost normal. It's time to check your wound, although I suspect you are well on the road to recovery. You're far too chipper this morning to be lying around in bed."

All the while she removed the bandage, cleaned the wound and covered it again with fresh sterile cloth, William watched her. It was unnerving, and she had to remind herself to focus on the task. His comments lightened the moment, and she found herself enjoying his banter.

"Shaky this morning, Miss Miller?"

"You, kind sir, would unsettle the nerves of a saint."

"And are you a saint?"

"Heavens no. I'm far too opinionated."

"Agreed. Your halo is a bit lopsided."

"You're confusing saints with angels. Are you a religious man, William?"

"Attended church weekly my entire life. Does that count?"

"You must know it does not, or you wouldn't ask."

"Let's say I have swayed occasionally from convictions promised at the altar of decision. My comrades in arms are a rowdy bunch."

"So, you are a follower? I'd have never guessed. But since we're on the topic of the men in St. Albans, it impressed me the way my assailants backed off when confronted about waylaying me. Yet, even now, when you agree they are an unruly bunch, you also admit to taking part in their behavior. I detect a great contradiction in your character. How do you sleep at night?"

He laughed aloud. "You boggle my mind with your reasoning. But dearest Emma, I fear the army ties my hands. We have our orders. The country is at war."

Her face contorted. "So, now I'm Emma?"

"In my mind, always." He grinned. "And if it

makes you feel better, I don't participate all the time, and when I must, it's never willingly."

"No, I'm afraid it does not make me feel better at all. A man should not have to compromise his values for the sake of obedience. But, William, I understand the need to obey one's higher-ranking officer, and will concede to allow you and the Good Lord to deal with your transgressions."

"Very gracious of you," he teased.

"No—gracious of God."

"And what of your family? Ethan is dead—are there others enlisted?"

"Two more, Mason and Henry. But strategic plans from generals got them killed as well. I have no siblings left." She passed him a cup of tea. "I should bring the tray downstairs and let you rest."

With his free hand, he reached out and grabbed her arm. "I've enjoyed our talk. I hope you don't hate me. You have provided the only bright spot in this entire war and it felt liberating to voice an opinion freely without threats of reprisal."

"Your silver tongue is on the loose again. Surely after forty-two long months, you have known brighter spots than visiting a farm girl in Vermont?"

"None that compares." He stared openly and its intensity demanded her full and undivided attention. "If I returned to the Miller farm after the war ends, would you welcome me as a friend, or perhaps a suitor?"

"You're delirious, Mr. Davis," Emma said.

"Then tell me—that James fella visiting here this morning—is he your beau?"

"He'd like to think he is." Emma shook her arm loose of his hold and picked up the tray of dishes. His face held a multitude of questions and she tried to imagine the possibility of a Southerner returning to call upon her. She pushed the idea away. "Your family in Kentucky will need you to return home and bring your plantation into the new era."

"Perhaps they will better listen to us?" William suggested. When Emma did not respond, he lowered his gaze to his cup and lifted it to his mouth. "But I am being far too forward. My apologies, Miss Miller."

Now that they were back on a last name basis, it was time to exit. "Rest. I will look in later." She started toward the door.

"I'll be gone when you return, Emma Miller. And know this, I will miss you terribly."

Refusing to look back in case her heart betrayed her, Emma closed the door with a gentle click then collapsed against the wall. Her head attempted to reason with her emotions, but neither won the ongoing battle. William made Emma feel alive on the inside, raw emotions she'd never before experienced but which now stirred within at the mere remembrance of him. His final words nagged at her mercilessly. He would do the honorable thing and slip away. While the offer warmed her heart, it also caused sadness. She sighed and forced her feet to descend the steps.

When Emma entered the kitchen, her father was sitting at the table, still clutching a full cup of coffee in his hand.

"Papa, I thought you had chores this morning?"

"Yes, chores. How could I forget?" He stood to his feet and walked to the door. She felt the cup, and it was stone cold.

Before he stepped outside, she yelled, "Put on your coat. You'll catch a death of foolishness." She watched him struggle and went to help. "Let me come with you. Maybe we'll stop by and pay our respects at the gravestones?"

"That'd be fine, daughter. I miss talking with your mama." No mention of Ethan. Somehow, she'd have to break through his confusion.

Chapter 7

TO THE RESCUE

Joseph stared at the freshly covered grave. His tormented face revealed the raging tides tossing inside the uncooperative mind. Emma's heart broke as she kneeled on the cold earth next to her father.

"Papa, the family is resting in the arms of Jesus. No more pain and think of the grand reunion. Mama loves to cook for the boys and is probably nagging them to take off their boots so as not to soil the gold floors in her new mansion."

"Your mama never cared about gold floors."

"Reverend Taplie says God promised we'd walk on gold, so that's what we get on the other side. No sense arguing with it." Emma hoped she recalled the sermon accurately.

"Suppose." His hand ran along the cross they'd erected to mark Ethan's grave. Emma held her breath and waited for him to speak. "Can't wrap my head around Ethan being gone. Far too young for the hereafter."

Emma gasped. So soon, Papa had forgotten the man upstairs who was hopefully planning to make his escape. The constant mix-up happening within his fragile mind pained her more than his earlier condition of natural grief. She did not pretend to understand the workings of the mind, but accepted that it was a complex creation designed by an all-knowing God. And not knowing how to fix his twisted condition, she chose not to add to his comment at all.

"Bess is almost ready to birth the new calf, Papa. Why don't you go check on her while I gather the eggs from the henhouse?"

"Grand idea, daughter. The barn is getting skimpy of animals these days—need to keep populating it if we're to survive." In the same breath, he brightened. "Maybe pluck us one of your prize-eating chickens for dinner tonight. You need to feed your brother quality food while he's home recuperating."

Emma sighed. His reality shifted again during the brief moments they'd kneeled by the graveside.

How would she cope?

Eggs were plentiful that morning, and it didn't take long to fill her basket. If only she could take them to town for Mr. Statford at the mercantile. They could use the trading power to stock up on supplies for the coming winter. Setting the bounty on the ground, she surveyed the four remaining meat chickens. She'd hoped to save them for leaner times but she'd not disappoint Papa, although she wondered if he'd even recall asking. Emma eyed them up, privately wishing William could be here for the evening feast. Should she have stopped him or at least given permission for him to return after the war ended? Her heart and mind suffered conflict like never before and her mother's words of old brought comfort. *The Good Lord has a plan, Emma, and if you're patient, the right path will unfold without the fuss of worrying.*

A loud noise in the direction of the barn drew her attention. Thoughts of her father sent her racing toward the building. When she saw riders, she slipped in along the side out of sight. She moved along the barn-board wall until she found her childhood snooping spot - a place where the panels separated and allowed viewing into the interior. She crouched and peered inside.

Joseph swayed on his feet while William held him upright against a center post. Beside him, slung over a rafter hung a long rope and even from her vantage point she saw the red raw ring around her father's throat. Could William be hanging her father? That seemed out of character, but perhaps his comrade standing at the door thought it jolly fun and William was succumbing to his *following-the-crowd* personality. Emma bit the back of her hand to stop the terrifying scream that longed to escape.

"You going soft on us, Davis? We both know your old man back home would frown on you disobeying an officer. Did I mention that he sent his regards last time we spoke?"

"Don't pretend to know what my father thinks, let alone that he'd care to send his regards through you."

"Ah, but you're wrong. Met him just six months ago. The man's taken a shine to me. Bet you didn't know he is a valuable influence in rallying Confederate sympathizers in our neighboring country to the north."

"My father focuses his vision on his enterprises in Kentucky. He'd never risk scandal to the Davis name; in Canada or anywhere, for that matter."

"You're out of touch, Willy-boy."

"Perhaps, but your questionable reputation with the home-crowd will not die anytime soon. My father holds grudges for a long time."

Yonge laughed. "The war broadens a man's thinking. You'd be amazed of the evil planned behind closed doors. And for your information, Theodore Davis approved you joining our little band of forward-thinkers, but the army put me in charge. So, you best not forget who wears the stripes."

Emma knew the man speaking. He'd entered the store while she was in town. Although young and ruggedly handsome, his countenance reeked of trouble. The condescending grin he aimed at William cut the air like a sharp sword. "Now, I've given you a loose rein, Will, because of our family bond, but the fellas in town aren't too happy with you throwing your weight around. Might have to pull in your reins to keep the boys happy." A few of the men behind him cheered agreement.

"Suit yourself. You've been good at keeping secrets from us, so why should I expect anything different?"

"You'll know the entire plan when it suits me and not a minute before. Is that clear, William?"

"Clear as mud."

"The boys are wondering why you're hiding out here. Some say this is where that young filly lives, the one selling the eggs at the store."

William never answered him directly but pointed to Joseph. "Had an accident in the woods and landed here, but the shoulder's mending fine now."

"Just the old man lives here, then?" Yonge asked.

William avoided the question. "Leave the old man alone. He's known enough grief."

"Like I said, you've gone soft, William. Recall a time back home when you did my bidding. Got me accepted into that inside circle with your precious group of snobby friends."

William cut him off. "A lot has happened since then, Bennett. You're talking foolish and you know it. Surely three years of this war has grown headstrong boys into wiser men."

The air hung thick, with emotion igniting every word. There appeared to be a peacemaker in the group who tried to pull the men off the fatal path their conversation headed. "You're bleeding," he announced while pointing toward William's stained shirt.

"It's nothing." William tucked in the gray shirt that had pulled loose then closed his jacket to cover the stain.

"Doctor in town will stitch you up," Bennett said.

"Been stitched up, just overdid myself out here in the barn."

All the while they talked, Joseph Miller gazed from one to the other, confused about the discussion and the men who stood in his barn. But the hanging still stumped Emma. The blood oozing from William's shirt suggested he'd overtaxed his wound and his friends from town had just newly arrived on the barn scene. So that only left one scenario. It sickened Emma to think her father might have sunk low enough to attempt suicide.

It was unthinkable.

"Well, I reckon we'll hang out here with you for a while. Change of scenery will do us good. And should the Union come checking on the old man while you're tucking him in, we'll be here to support you in the fight." The men roared with laughter.

The leader wore authority like a trophy and defied William to contradict him. Emma could see William's struggle.

"How's the arm, William?" Emma recognized the speaker as one of the riff-raff who'd confronted her that day in town. "Thought I saw Avis head this way, hot on the scent of the egg-toting farm girl. Might take a mosey around the place; see if he got lost."

"I've been around," William said. "He should have thought twice about wandering in woods where he doesn't belong."

"Need to clean my gun, anyway. Been acting up lately and liable to shoot itself off without me pulling the trigger."

After the words spewed from his mouth, Emma watched the hard lines form on William's face. The two men stared, the unspoken challenge sealing the connection.

"Now calm down, boys," Bennett said. "We've a job to do, and then you can both kill each other for all I care. All the more plunder for me."

"There's no need to bother the old man any further, Lieutenant," William said using a new tone of respect. "Let's go back to town. Was on my way there before you arrived." He pushed forward as if to lead the group from off the property.

"Hold up, Davis! I don't think we'll be going anywhere just yet. You're far too eager. We best stick around and see what you're up to."

"Nothing here but an old man," William said, his eyes resting on Joseph. Emma saw the turmoil in his face. His attempt to protect her did not go unappreciated.

"Surely there's a proper cook stove and a full pantry for Jed to feed us a decent meal. Or better yet, why don't you go kill us some meat, William? Blow off some steam and get that shooting arm active again," Bennett said in a tone not open for debate.

"Let me settle the old man in his room first, then I'll scare us up some grub."

"Yeah, you do that, Willy-boy," cooed the

bully she recalled from town.

Emma wondered if William suspected she'd overheard their plans from the safety of her hiding place. He had not mentioned her—clearly hoping to keep her out of harm's way. Forced to trust William to watch out for her father's safety while she ran for help, she stood to her feet.

Before the men left the barn, Emma hurried to the tree line and disappeared behind it. She glanced back and viewed the exodus of six men headed toward the house. Joseph followed William's lead, but she feared for the emptiness she saw in his eyes. Unrest filled Emma's heart. The Union soldiers were long gone and if she brought a posse from town and they charged the gang at the hill farm, William might die in the battle. The ache that settled deep inside answered the questions that plagued her—she cared for the Confederate soldier—probably more than she should. She'd wait a few minutes with hopes to speak to him when he came out again to hunt supper.

Only one of Yonge's men remained outside and sprawled in her father's rocking chair on the porch. He leaned his head back and instantly fell asleep on his watch. No wonder the Confederates were losing the war.

Ten minutes later, the door opened again and William appeared with his rifle in hand. He looked around the yard and headed off toward the henhouse, probably the last place he'd seen her go. Emma weaved through the bushes and trees and landed at the back around the same time he entered the tree line.

The worry lines on his face disappeared as he rushed toward her. "Emma, thank God you're safe."

"I am, and so is my father, thanks to you. I appreciate you seeing him to his room. Hopefully, he stays there."

He searched her face and then asked, "Did you hear what went on in the barn?"

"I saw your friends and heard the plan to hole up in the house for a spell. I figured it best to run for help, but then heard you'd be coming hunting, so waited to speak with you first. William, I don't want to bring the war to my farmhouse and..."

He stepped closer. "And what?"

"I don't want Union supporters to kill you." Her face turned beet-red, but she rambled on. "Is that what you want to hear? That I'm a traitor and care far too much for one Rebel soldier to watch him die on my doorstep!"

Emma's voice rose and William closed the gap between them laying a hand across her mouth. He glanced behind him but no movement stirred from inside the house or from the man on the porch.

Slowly he withdrew his hand, but it lingered

and crept behind her braid to the back of her neck. Ever so gently he drew her head toward him. Their eyes held and Emma could no more resist the tenderness of this man than she could a brand-new kitten in the barn. William wore his heart openly for her to view and she surrendered to the gentle brush of his lips on hers. After a brief, tantalizing search, he withdrew, and she heard the deep groan of her name, "Emma." She rested her head against his chest and abandoned all common sense in his embrace. She responded to his kisses knowing the enemy had stolen her heart.

William gently pushed her to arm's length. "Emma. I never planned for this to happen. You're so easy to love."

"Nor did I, William Davis. It appears you also have been the only bright spot I've known in over three years. And I'll not scold myself for grabbing a passing ray of sunshine while shrouded in a black cloud of wartime."

"Is that all I mean to you? A kiss to pass the time?"

"I've known you two days. What more can there possibly be? Besides, you are from the South and I, the North. This cursed war spoiled our chances long before we ever met."

"The war will be over soon. You said so yourself."

"And then what? You will move to Vermont and live as a farmer with my father and me?"

"Or you and your father can travel south—live on a plantation with servants and never want for anything again."

"Servants or slaves? You've hit on the very core of what separates us. I will never allow someone to sacrifice their life to make me comfortable and lazy."

William smiled. "One of the qualities I love most about you. Independent, hardworking, and kind."

"That's more than one, sir," Emma said.

"Don't get me on a roll. I have a lot more praise to send your way."

"Perhaps the best we can do is see what happens when you return for that visit after the war."

"Ah, ha. So now I'm invited?"

"You are invited."

"What of your Union man James?"

"James was my brother's best buddy, an old family friend, and a good neighbor. Mind you, I get the impression from his recent visits that he'd like to pursue something more permanent after the war." Emma smiled mischievously. "Guess I'll see who arrives on my doorstep first." She meant it as a joke, but the panic growing in William's face revealed that he'd missed the banter. She leaned over and planted a light kiss on the lips that still burned with the passion of moments earlier. She forced herself to pull back.

"Relax, William Davis. You are by far the better kisser."

Chapter 8

DISCOVERED

"Now, what do we have here?"

William and Emma separated and stared into the leering face of the man that had awakened from his snooze on the porch. They'd lingered too long, enjoying sinful pleasures of the stolen moment. William squeezed her hand.

"We met up in the woods, Jed. I'm heading off to get meat for supper now."

"Maybe the fellas would like a taste of the little gal you found? You can't be hogging the merchandise for yourself."

William stepped forward and loomed over the

man. "This girl is not up for grabs. I told you that once before and I'll not be telling you again. You can find the sort you crave in town at the saloon. Help yourself."

"The lieutenant might have something different to say about it."

"Over my dead body."

"If I looked in the forest here, would I find Avis' body?" Jed sneered. "Tell you what, give me the girl and you can keep your secrets."

"No deal."

"You're a long way from home, William, and the wealthy Theodore Davis is not here to purchase this piece of merchandise for you."

William's fist shot out and sent the man wheeling backward but he stayed on his feet. Emma gasped and quickly moved in between them, her glare focused on Jed. "This merchandise is not for sale—now or ever. And you are despicable!" She picked up her skirt and started to move deeper into the woods.

"Where do you think you're going?" Jed asked while wiping a trickle of blood from his mouth.

"William's arm is still healing. I will help him shoot meat for your supper just to get you out of my kitchen and off my land. The ravages of war have turned you into a loathsome human being."

He roared laughing. "Willy-boy. You got yourself a spitfire and her hair isn't even cherry red like the sweetie waiting at home for you."

Emma bit her lip to stop it from quivering. She had risked her virtue to a man promised to another woman. Emma turned fiery eyes on William. "And you are the worst of the lot." His eyes softened, and she witnessed his silent pleading, but her anger within did not subside.

No one followed as she marched off. Perhaps she should run to town and stick with the original plan. Let the posse invade and clean the world of these shameful creatures. Tears flowed freely, and she cursed her newfound weakness. A woman was better and stronger alone. Her solitary walk ended abruptly when William whirled her around to face him.

"You can't leave now. Jed will brag about his find to all the men. If I don't return with you and the meat, he's threatened your father. He comes from Kentucky too – one of Yonge's followers from way back. The wild boy grew into a rowdy man. I'm sorry."

Emma believed he meant it. "Good thing you're sorry about something, Mr. Davis."

"I'm not sorry about the kiss. Are you?"

"Your little redhead at home would not appreciate hearing you say that," Emma said lifting her chin in defiance.

"Rosalie? She's nothing to me. She prances around the plantation like she expects a future there, but the only thing that really lights up her eyes is old money built from generations of hard-working Davis men. And don't look at me like that. They may use slaves for the ground work, but it takes an enterprising man to build a legacy."

Emma backed off. "I never meant to imply that your family did not work. Success involves a multitude of talents."

"Thank you. And what of the other?"

"The girl who pines for you at home? I suppose you shall have to see if she still waits for her moneyman to return from war. A promise is a promise."

"I never promised her anything. You must believe me."

"Why must I believe anything the enemy says? We are at war, William Davis, and if you plan on living to see its end, I suggest you choose sides and fight for what you believe. Or continue to ride out your yellow-belly carcass on the back of a Rebel horse." Emma moved deeper into the brush. "Come on. I'll show you my favorite spot. Always meat waiting there for the Miller's table."

Back at the ranch, Emma pounded and kneaded the dough, setting pans on the warming tray to rise. She'd kicked everyone out of the kitchen except Jed, who refused to go claiming his status as Yonge's cook, although she doubted his devotion to the task. She plunked a pail of potatoes in front of him. "Peel these." He grabbed at her wrist and she shook free. "And don't touch me ever again."

The anger fueling Emma's insides allowed her to talk boldly and display a brave front. If it weren't for her father lying quietly upstairs, she'd throw herself in front of a bullet before she'd feed the likes of these men. They were the lowest of all soldiers, traitors and cowards to their own flag, hiding out in Vermont's most northern town disguised as sportsmen. A scattered group, as they'd arrived from different locations, but all playing the king-card to a bunch of farmers and business owners that had mostly escaped the ravages of the war in their hometown. Big men! She felt like spitting in their faces. And the worst thing of all was that she'd flaunted herself shamelessly before one of them.

Still, her heart fought for the man. It was hard to throw him in with the rabble-rousers he rode with. He stuck out like a lone flower in amongst a patch of weeds. She continually forced her thoughts to turn against him—it was her only hope to survive the heartbreak of his betrayal. No matter how kind he'd been to her family in standing against his own to defend hers, he'd been out of line to act upon his feelings for her. A lonely woman waited at home for his return. A vision of James sprang into her mind and suddenly her childhood friend emerged the better contender for a future husband. She'd do well to stick to her own kind. At least he was a solid, loyal man, even if his presence did nothing to arouse the womanly side of her. The next time he came calling at the farm, she swore she'd throw herself into his arms and summon that same passion she'd felt with William. Mind over heart. Maybe then it wouldn't hurt so much to say goodbye to the Southerner who'd invaded her soul.

A soldier delivered the prepared steaks to the back door and Emma threw them into the frying pans. Recalling the care she'd taken for the dinner she'd served the Union soldiers added fuel to the fire inside her.

This bunch would not eat so well.

Emma added no seasoning to lessen the wild taste of the meat, for the sorry lot had cut dinner from the wrong section of the deer. The result would be tough and chewy. The innate desire to please those who sat at her table opposed her, and giving in, she chopped onions and mushrooms to fry as a side dish. She pulled the basket of large over-ripened carrots that she'd stashed in the back corner of her upstairs storeroom—declaring them uneatable—and cut them into chunks, determined to cook the life out of them.

Finally, Jed finished peeling the potatoes and she added his contribution to boiling water.

Emma stoked the fire and prayed they'd devour the meal quickly and bring a quick end to the invasion of her home.

Bored with watching Emma work, Jed left to join the others on the porch. Ten minutes later, William wandered in through the back door and silently crept in behind Emma as she mashed the potatoes. She jumped when she felt his touch, and with no place to move, gritted her teeth and waited for him to speak.

"Emma, I'll bring a plate to your father and make sure he eats."

She wilted. Just when she'd convinced herself of his worthlessness, he wanted to serve her father supper. This man wore a dozen faces and Emma's confusion rose to her cheeks. She reached to the side and grabbed a plate from the stack. "Thank you, Mr. Davis. I would appreciate that."

"Enough to give me the hope of a smile?" he asked.

She bit her lip and turned to face him, full plate in hand. "Will you be eating upstairs as well?"

His expression drooped, and he nodded. "Suppose I could, but I wanted to be sure the men didn't give you a hard time at supper."

"I can look after myself. No need to concern yourself with my well-being."

"But I am concerned. Just because you're angry doesn't change my feelings for you."

"I promise to yell if anyone gets out of hand. Does that meet your approval?"

"Please, Emma." She shoved the plate into his chest. "Let me make up a second. You can pour coffee and grab a couple slices of bread. It may be the only thing that saves the meal."

"Oh? Not taking pride in feeding the enemy?"

"Not one bit."

"You didn't poison it, did you?" William winked to lighten the mood.

"Now why didn't I think of that? I know exactly where to find some poison mushrooms." Emma said this as she scooped some of her fried mixture onto the side of their plates. William raised his eyebrows and stared. She couldn't help but laugh. "Do you honestly think I'd kill my own father?"

"Good point." He glanced up and their eyes held. Emma did not back down. "I wonder if Papa still thinks you're Ethan?"

"Not sure. He's not talking much but I hope to start a good conversation during dinner."

"And will you tell him he's eating with a traitor?"

"Whoever I am to you, he understands that I

saved his life from the brink of death. That will either give me favor with the man or provide the ammunition to throw me to the wolves like his daughter is doing."

"That's not true. I harbor no wish for harm to find you. This war has torn our country to pieces and I truly hope you survive to help rebuild your world - as I will mine."

"With James? Somehow I believe you are planning to settle with leftovers."

"James is a good man and will make a fine husband."

"Yes—for someone who loves him! Don't give the man any less than that. From what you say, he deserves the best future possible." He turned and picked up the tray they'd been filling, and headed for the stairs.

Emma kicked the stove leg, hard. Why did he have to say that? She was more than aware that her love for James did not carry with it the emotions designed for a married couple, and no amount of kissing to prove otherwise would stir it up. She recalled her mother's words, *the perfect man will sweep you off your feet,* and Emma knew beyond a doubt that William fit those requirements. Her shoulders sagged as she pictured her new future as a spinster. At least she'd secured the memory of one great kiss to take the pain away but with it, the ache magnified.

Emma carried a basin of water, a bar of soap and a towel to the veranda. She ignored the whistles and placed hands on her hips to help make her point clear to the men who littered her front entranceway. "Wash up for dinner, gentlemen," she said, nearly choking on the suggestion that these soldiers possessed any gentlemanly qualities. "If you have plates and cups in your sacks, bring them along or you'll eat in shifts. I don't have settings for everyone." She probably did but refused to contaminate her dishes.

They trampled in, one by one, with tin cups and plates, a fork and a knife, which Emma felt certain, sliced more than food. They perched on the edge of chairs around the table as men trained to flee at a moment's notice. The scene sickened her, and she yearned to bury her head in a pillow and let the tears flow. Not long ago, her brothers and parents had occupied this kitchen as a family and as her heart yearned to hide in the quiet place where her father found comfort, she rallied instead, and enabled the strong woman to break loose from the cocoon of her childhood shell.

Emma's stance did not encourage conversation of any kind, and thankfully no one spoke. Bowls of lumpy potatoes, old earth-tainted carrots, and fried vegetables lined the center. Platters of the fresh, tough meat, thin slices of day-old bread and a dish of butter joined the choices. No pickles or yummy-tasting dessert would find their way into the mouths of these scoundrels. Emma wiped wet hands on her apron, poured a cup of coffee, and headed for the stairs.

"Where are you going?" Bennett Yonge yelled out.

"Upstairs to tend my father." She didn't bother to inform him William was already there. She'd relieve the man so he could come and sit with his own kind.

Chapter 9

THE TRUTH COMES OUT

When Emma entered the room, her father brightened and slapped the bed sheets beside him. "Come sit, daughter. Judging by the taste of this grub you whipped up, I'm thinking you need a rest. Must have exhausted you to spoil God's provisions this badly."

Joseph Miller laughed and Emma sat, not sure if he reprimanded or complimented her on a foiled job well done. William's grin reached across the bed and tore down her defensive walls in one easy sweep. She despised the telltale smile that reached her face in response.

"That's more like it," Joseph said, patting his

daughter's arm. "Now, down to business. How do we get rid of the riff-raff invading our house?" He looked toward William for the answer and Emma did likewise.

"I hope they won't stay long. Maybe we should ride it out—be the best hosts we can. If they'd planned any mischief, they'd have done it by now."

"Maybe they're waiting until after they fill their stomachs," Emma suggested.

"Yeah, well, the outhouse will be busy tonight if they stay over," Joseph said rather jovially, and both men chuckled at his sitting rendition of a bull-legged man headed for the privy.

"Surely they won't sleep here with perfectly fine beds in town," Emma said, exasperated at the thought of Rebels under her roof. She glanced at the uncertainty in William's eyes and muttered, "Cursed war! James thinks the end is near, maybe even before Christmas. Hopefully, that news will make the freezing Confederates happy enough to go home and leave us be."

Joseph agreed with a calm spirit. "That way they can not only surrender to the Union but to the love born in a stable. Great time to accept His gift of salvation and ask forgiveness from the Babe in the Manger for the monstrosities inflicted while enslaving their fellow man."

William coughed and glanced at Emma over

the top of his hand. He steered clear of a religious reference. "I'm afraid the other side disagrees concerning your timetable. Southerners can be stubborn to the bitter end."

"And you'd surely know, boy," Joseph said, his generous expression providing Emma no clue who he envisioned the man sitting next to him to be.

Emma stammered, unsure how to address William in the presence of her father. Was he the hated Confederate soldier tonight or the beloved son Ethan? She studied Joseph Miller. Physically he appeared normal, but she'd seen his mind lose focus in an instant, and this caused her added concern with the enemy loitering in their home.

She'd let the men lead the conversation and raised the cup of coffee to her lips. The first sip caused her face to grimace. The men roared with laughter. Somehow she'd spoiled the coffee without even trying. It must be the root of bitterness that invaded the entire meal, and that realization did not provide comfort. Far too much repentance was on the horizon, for surely this horrid war had affected everyone in the country, including her.

"Let me change your bandage," Emma said, rising and going to a nearby chest of drawers. She opened it and withdrew clean dressings. At the basin, she drenched a washcloth and walked toward William. "Please, remove your shirt."

He stood to do her bidding, and as each button loosened, the staring between the two intensified. Emma scolded herself for caring one smidgen about infection spoiling the soft skin hiding beneath the fabric. But she'd already crossed all emotional barriers with this man and sealed her fate. She'd just begun cleaning the dried blood around the wound when the door was flung open and a smug Bennett Yonge leaned against the frame.

"Now, isn't this a cozy scene?"

Emma continued her work, refusing to fall prey to his bullying. "You are not welcome here, sir. Is there something you require in the kitchen?"

"Why no, pretty lady. All the men's tummies are full, thanks to you. Now they're hankering entertainment." He winked at Emma, who unconsciously sunk her fingernails into William's shoulder. She heard the patient's faint gasp and smiled weakly. The man at the door laughed in a disgusting manner. "Relax, farm girl. The men have their sites set on the painted ladies in town. Some might stay overnight but I doubt it. Most of us are heading back. But I'd keep my doors locked tonight if I were you—just in case."

Emma wondered why William didn't speak up, then remembered her father who'd gone silent again. His consideration to avoid a scene added one more nail to her coffin of romantic regrets. Without even trying, William Davis continued to win her affections at every turn and her hands shook as she laid the clean bandage next to the open wound. The skin surrounding it showed good color and the healing process was right on schedule.

The voice on the other side of the room shattered the carefully built wall of protection that she and William had erected for her father.

"So, Willy-boy, you joining the fun or staying to babysit the farmers?"

"I'm staying," William said.

"Suit yourself," Jed said you had eyes for the girl but I didn't believe it until now. She doesn't hold a candle to Rosalie," Bennett said.

Yonge's horrid laugh echoed down the hall as he made his way to the stairs. Emma raced to the door and slammed it shut. She leaned against it and closed her eyes. When she opened them, William stood in front of her.

"Are you all right?"

"Fine." She gathered her strength and added, "Glad to see the last of that lot."

"Gather your night things and move into this room tonight. I'll drag in a mattress for you and when it comes sleeping time, I'll stretch my blanket across the outside. No one will get past me. You can rest in peace."

"Why do you care?"

"I think I made that abundantly clear earlier, Miss Miller." His voice was intimate and low. Emma flattened herself against the door.

"I do appreciate your help, sir, but that is all there will ever be between us. You know that, right?"

"Ah yes, because of the redhead." William grinned and Emma was aghast.

"You make light of it, as if she doesn't matter."

"She doesn't—and never did. You've chosen to embellish a lie spoken from a spiteful enemy. I'd hoped to measure higher on your scale of people to respect than Bennett Yonge."

A voice from the bed shook their not-so private moment. "I may be old but I'm not deaf, I think some truth is in order tonight."

Emma bit her lip and William squeezed her hand. "Truth is always the best route, Emma. Now would be a good time to trust your God."

They walked toward the bed, William gripping her hand hard so she could not pull free.

"Yes, sir," William began. "Shall we place all our cards on the table tonight?"

"You're a Johnny Reb, aren't you? Thought I recognized the gray duds but the fabric's all tattered and torn like a man who's crawled through too many bushes and creeks." Joseph put his hand into the air to stop William's interruption. "Besides, that accent you try to hide hit the air singing when you cut me down from the rafter." He looked at Emma. "I'm sorry, daughter. The futility of bad news all sort of took me over. Not proud of the act."

"I'm glad to hear we won't be enduring that again anytime soon," Emma said.

"Not my time. Told your Mama that very thing, and she seems willing to wait. This fella reminded me I have a daughter who loves me and needs me. It shames me to think I might have left you at the mercy of these scoundrels. Course I never imagined there was any hand-holding going on between him and you." Joseph stared at the man, who refused to let go of Emma. "Think it's about time you introduced yourself and stated your intentions, mister."

"My name is William Davis from Kentucky, sir. My family has owned a prosperous plantation for generations and when I left, we numbered six boys and two girls at home. One brother is dead, but I truly hope the rest find their way home after the war."

"I had three boys—all dead, fighting for the cause—and a wife whose heart split open with grief. All's left is Emma and me, and this hill farm that's provided a good livelihood for us over the years."

"I am sorry for your losses, sir." William released Emma's hand and stepped closer. "I need you to understand this war has never been my fight. I loathe slavery. One of my best-kept secrets is a friendship I share with the son of our blacksmith. He works the fields with a spirit that surpasses the high-and-mighty upper class my father would have me embrace. Course none of that matters for I am Confederate in name and rank and have fought your countrymen to the death on many occasions."

Joseph winked at his daughter. "Honesty—ain't that one of your musts for a good man?"

"Yes Papa, but…"

"Hush now. I want to hear his story."

William continued. "My efforts to break free of my family's political viewpoint was impossible and after a year of fighting in the South, I gave up my rank as an officer and joined the first regiment headed north. Figured if I got far enough, I'd slip across the border and wait it out. Perhaps a coward's way out, but necessary to keep my sanity intact."

At that point, a shadow fell across his face and Emma witnessed him battle with how much truth it required to satisfy her father. His following words left a gap in his story—she was certain of it. "Seemed lots of men had the same idea. Once discovered, the army ordered me to join a new command that unfortunately turned out to be drifters seeking personal gain amid all this bloodshed. Greed and pride govern their hearts and I find myself in a peculiar situation, at odds with my conscience."

"You speak of personal gain. Is such a thing possible, or do you refer to money received from sporting events?" Emma asked.

She watched him squirm. "Yes, apparently men are profiting in both areas. The lieutenant doesn't divulge his plans too far in advance. He's a secretive sort."

"Bennett Yonge appears to know you well enough," Emma stated as if that qualified him as a close confidante.

"He's an acquaintance from my home state. That's all."

"So how does a man profit from the hardships of war?" asked Joseph.

"Always money to make when you know how."

"And you know how?" Emma asked.

"Appears my new commander is an expert. Got enormous amounts stashed in Canadian banks. Of course, they hand over a mere pittance for the Confederate treasury to keep the generals off their trail, but most will return home wealthy men."

"And what do you want here in St. Albans?"

"I don't know, Emma—truly. I'm hoping we're just planning sporting events, but I doubt it. Yonge chooses his time to share. For him, it's all about controlling others."

"Emma, did you expect the soldier to tell us what the Rebs are planning? That would be a far worse crime than being a traitor to the Union flag."

William raised his eyebrows and Emma detected a touch of humor in his face, for Emma had declared that very loyalty statement to him earlier.

She peered at her father. "I said the exact thing to William recently."

"It is disconcerting to have the bunch so close knowing they have treachery up their sleeve," Joseph said. "With James gone, they've got free reign."

"Now who's telling secrets?" Emma asked.

Joseph tossed the cover off. "I'm tired of hiding out in this room."

"All is safe with me. I wish I could disappear, but they court-marshal soldiers for desertion, and I don't relish dying during or after the war." William turned to Emma. "Especially now."

"Aha. So that brings us back to your intentions toward my daughter," Joseph said standing erect, all his mental faculties clear and focused.

William grasped Emma's wrists and pulled

her closer. "Your daughter has swept me off my feet, and I fear no matter where my future steps take me, I will falter without her by my side." Emma looked to the floor, unable to hold his gaze. He raised his finger and tipped her chin upward. "She suspects I have a future in Kentucky teaching my war-defeated kin how to run a business without the aid of slave labor." A grin covered his face. "She also suspects that a redheaded female pines for my safe return. When in truth, Rosalie's sole objective is to gain social recognition as Mrs. William Davis, the wife of a wealthy landowner—a title she can rub into the faces of her competition." His smile expanded when he noticed the tiniest hint of a grin toying at the corner of Emma's lips.

She couldn't allow the last remark to go unchallenged. "Competition? My oh my, so you are a sought-after man, are you Mr. Davis?"

"You, Emma Miller, have nothing to fear from the ladies of Kentucky. It appears your jealousy is the only competition that continues to stand in our way."

All set to protest his remark, Joseph's belly laugh caught her by surprise. Her jaw dropped. "What's so funny?"

"Watching you two gives an old man hope. You're the spitting image of your mama, girl and you've a temper to match." He moved closer to confront William. "Young man, I sure hope you haven't bitten off more than you can chew." He offered William a handshake. "The heart doesn't know the difference between North and South. Love trots from state to state on a whim, unaffected by the boundaries men set in place. Good luck, Mr. Davis."

Flabbergasted, Emma cried, "Are you in your right mind, Papa?"

"If you mean, have I settled that your man here is not your brother Ethan? Then yes, I'm in my right mind, and plan on staying in the land of the living until the Good Lord calls me home, natural-like."

Emma twisted to find William continuing his intense search of her, his eyes begging acceptance. After a moment, he spoke. "So, Miss Miller, will you keep company with me or James after the war ends?"

"William, I refuse to leave my father and go south, and although we are a generous bunch, you will find it difficult to fit in with Northerners."

"You are the one who keeps suggesting that my future is southbound. I would be content to farm this land with you and your father. The hills will keep the homesickness at bay and I'm certain, given time, your neighbors will forget I am an outsider. I will work hard to *fit in,* Emma Miller."

"But we are far from rich, William, and it's hard work to turn a profit on a small farm."

"Have you not been listening? I am the rebellious son of Theodore Davis. Never wanted wealth and all the stuffy expectations that accompany it."

Emma joined in the compromise while she inched closer to William. "I suppose your brothers will gladly swallow up your share of the family inheritance."

"Gladly, and not miss me for a moment."

Emma bent in and kissed his cheek. "Well, Mr. Davis, I shall expect you to call at the Miller farm after the first sign of surrender."

William's eyes twinkled. "So sure of a Union win, aren't you, Miss Miller?"

"Most definitely—and soon. I'm not getting any younger."

Joseph Miller's voice boomed from his new position in front of the window. "Hurry up and give the girl a proper kiss, man. It's a long winter."

William did not have to be told twice. He pulled Emma into his arms and covered her lips with his. When he let her up for air, Emma's eyes filled with happy tears. He wiped them dry with a lone finger and kissed every inch of her face as delicately as a butterfly fluttering in the breeze.

"I am the happiest man in the country, Emma, and will count the days until we can be together as man and wife."

She stammered. "Another effort at a proposal, Mr. Davis?"

"I shall do much better when I return. Count on it."

Chapter 10

BUTTER DAY

No trouble erupted from the uninvited guests that night in the farmhouse, and when Emma went downstairs, she was ecstatic to see that all the men had returned to town at some point in the night. The three of them spent a perfect day together. Bessie gave birth to a healthy calf, and they picnicked for supper at Emma's favorite spot on the banks of Lake Champlain. All the while they laughed and talked, Emma sensed William's unrest. Despite his eagerness of yesterday to stay separated from his friends, he itched to return to town and did so the following day. He returned for hours on end, even helped Joseph with odd jobs on the farm. With boyish charm, the man proudly announced how he enjoyed the physical labor, the freedom of working outside in the fresh air, but mostly the feeling of accomplishment that a few hours of hard sweat provided a man. Everything seemed perfect in Emma's world, and she gladly pushed away impeding thoughts of war that still raged beyond her laneway.

October 18th was the day the community patiently awaited each year. A chance to show off their best work and provide needed commodities to their neighbors. A final opportunity to add a sizeable amount of cash to their bank accounts, money that would see them through the long cold winter. Emma was excited about the trip to town. She missed her friends and normal pre-war activity. She'd filled baskets with eggs, cheese, cream, and a separate one for her special fragrant soap that the hotels loved to purchase. In cartons she stacked preserves, and piled all the pumpkins and squash that remained in her garden. All of it sat by the door, ready for the trip to town.

Anticipation for the festivities, soon to spark new life in St. Albans, was clear from the glow on Emma's face and the celebratory spirit hung in the air like Christmas tinsel.

How Emma wished she could see the same enjoyment in William's face. The foul mood that descended on him at a moment's notice surely resulted from a stressful relationship with his town companions. She knew nothing of their hold on him.

And despite her best efforts to forget, the war continued to rage, conflicts both on the inside and the outside. James had spoken of an urgency that hovered in the camps, expecting upcoming battles before the snows came and the cold season forced troops to bunker down. Every day the papers wrote accounts of action happening somewhere in the country.

Emma heard William arrive on horseback and went outside to meet him. He tied his mare to the hitching post and jumped the stairs two at a time, pulling her into his arms.

"Town is already hopping, folks out and about. Couldn't wait to come see you."

"You certainly won't get a break from the crowds today. But tomorrow, forty of the villages leading men, including the county sheriff, will be off to Burlington for a Supreme Court hearing, or to Montpelier at the Legislature. But today, everyone stays home and gathers in St. Albans for Butter Day."

"I'll be looking forward to tomorrow then." Apparently, his day was not off to a good start. Emma ignored whatever he harbored beneath his hesitant tone. She was ready for this day – a much-needed ray of hope cast across a dark world.

"Don't despair. In the morning, you'll be able to shoot a cannon down the streets and not hit anyone. But on this special day, people will line the avenues to celebrate and share the harvest."

"Today? Why today?"

"Because it's always been today," Emma said with annoyance in her voice. "Don't be such a down-and-outer. It just so happens my stall is one of the favorite stops in the entire event. Allows me a great opportunity to meet up with friends." She spun on her toes and headed back inside, calling, "Papa, are you almost ready?"

"Yes, daughter," he said, as he passed her in the kitchen. "On the way to the barn as we speak. I'll bring the wagon around shortly." Joseph grabbed his hat and jacket off the hook and nodded. "Morning, William." Then he added, "It's chilly, Emma. Dress warm."

Emma detected distress in William's feeble response to her father's greeting and twirled around to confront him. His confusing stance startled her and again that nagging doubt seeped into her heart. "You are attempting to hide your secrets from me again."

William sighed. "It's war, Emma."

"Are you sure it's war and not cold feet, William? Perhaps you regret the words of love you promised to me?"

"I don't, Emma! But the men…"

"Are men so consumed with themselves that they leave no time for a man to heal from his wound?" Even as she said it, Emma knew that was a stretch, for William's arm healed at a miraculous rate. She tried another argument. "I'm sure your cohorts have no qualms visiting women they fancy whenever Bennett Yonge and the planning committee does not require an appearance."

William bypassed her objections and his answer was cool and detached. "I'm feeling better now, thanks to your nursing skills, and after today I won't be back for a long time."

Emma gulped. "That's rather sudden. The group has concluded their business meetings in St. Albans?"

"Almost. Today should put the final touches on the deal."

"You claim to have misgivings about the activities of your so-called sports buddies, so why should you waste time and effort in a project you have no heart for?"

"I'm expected to take part." She witnessed the darkness in his eyes and alerted to something new in his expression—fear.

She pushed past him, annoyed at the way this group of men worked. "Today is Butter Day and Papa and I will attend. You can do as you please."

"Butter Day should not be today!"

Emma halted in her preparations wondering about his sudden concern for the day. "It is, sir, and if you don't stop bellyaching, my customers will show up before I do."

William backed off. "I know I can say nothing to change your mind in attending so I won't try. Let's get that wagon packed. I need to speak to Yonge."

Suddenly, William was all hands on, helping to drag the containers onto the porch. His peculiar manner baffled her. It appeared Emma had given her heart to a stranger whose buddies proved the more important ones. Thankful to see this horrid flaw in William, she lifted her chin and worked side by side in silence.

Most of these visitors had occupied St. Albans for over a week now. The community as a whole accepted and interacted with them, and their conduct had proven gentlemanly – for the most part – causing only slight disturbances that seemed to follow men wherever they traveled. She pondered the true purpose for their staying on. The snippets of information William had alluded to, only fed her doubts. Dwelling on it always brought a suspicion to her mind that perhaps these friends – also branded Confederates – were in Vermont on duty. Was it sports or some war plan they discussed?

When she couldn't handle the suspense a moment longer, she blurted out, "William, has Bennett Yonge gathered you all here to plan an act of war?"

William remained quiet and withdrawn but she'd noticed a tiny twist of anguish cross his face like a storm brewing in the evening sky.

"Surely, as a loyal Union supporter, I should warn the authorities," Emma said.

That brought a response. "Please, Emma. Stay out of it. If you ever trusted me, do so now. I'd appreciate time spent on your knees, not any direct involvement. I have this under control."

"Why should I trust a Rebel who keeps secrets?"

"Because I love you, Emma Miller, and I hoped you saw beyond the color of the uniform."

"These men—and you for that matter—none of you wear uniforms. How are townsfolk supposed to know they are entertaining the enemy?"

He reached out and touched Emma's arm. "Please, Emma, trust your heart and your God. He will not lead you wrong."

Joseph Miller yelled from the yard as the wagon pulled up in front of the house. "Let's get loaded! Time to go." Joseph's sudden impatience rang loud and clear throughout his timbre.

Emma turned to face William and with as firm a voice as she could muster said, "Goodbye, William Davis. Perhaps you should return to Kentucky where you belong."

Emma didn't wait for a response and fled the house.

The tables sat waiting for Emma's market items and the town swarmed with people eager to begin the festive event. Although repeat customers flocked to her display, knowing she provided good product for hard-earned dollars, and new customers browsed, she kept an eye to the sidelines for anything that might hint at some sinister plan from the newcomers to St. Albans.

Emma noticed her best friend approaching. "Mary! It's so nice to see you. It's been ages. Is your brother over the croup?"

"Finally. Night duty is exhausting. I could barely put one foot in front of another most days." She bent low and spoke. "I was so sorry to hear about Ethan. You must be broken-hearted, suffering all the losses you have."

"We get through it, one day at a time."

"James told me about the funeral when we met up at the mercantile a few days back. He was buying supplies for his troops." She whispered, "I think he's smitten with you, Emma."

"Oh, Mary. My heart is not ready to love." A soon as she voiced it, she felt the rebuke. Love was not the issue—James was. But at that moment, Bennett Yonge slithered up behind Mary and all charitable thoughts banished.

"Good morning," he said to Mary. He tipped his hat and bowed in her direction. "The name is Bennett Henderson Yonge, at your service, ladies," he added, while including Emma in the scope of his introduction.

How ludicrous! She knew more than she cared to about the arrogant man and resented his coming around. But it appeared Mary did not. She turned a bright red and fanned her face when the ruggedly handsome chap targeted his attention back in her direction.

A figure stepped out from behind Yonge, and Emma gasped. Mary briefly noted him and returned her focus to Bennett.

He removed his hat. "My name is William Davis, if anyone is interested." He directed the comment to her as an attempt at humor. "Came to check out what you ladies are selling." He knew the inventory full well as he'd helped pile it in the wagon earlier, before taking off at a full gallop toward town.

Mary clued in to the new stranger's conversation. "Not me, sir! Heaven forbid. My mother says I am useless with anything that doesn't live in the barn."

William picked up a jar of jam. "How much for the spread?"

Emma puckered her lips. "The price is on the tag."

He looked down and smiled. "So it is." He reached into his pocket, withdrew some coins, and threw them on the table. "Keep the change." He looked at Emma but showed no recognition while the crimson color of her heart flooded her cheeks. Bennett Yonge noticed and couldn't resist commenting.

"Hey Willy, keep your hands off this new young filly. She's mine." He turned to wink at Emma. "You can have the farm girl—already tried making an impression on that one." His phony grin sickened Emma. He turned back to Mary. "What did you say your name was, sweetheart?" They marched across the grass, hand in hand.

Scooping the money off the table, Emma put it in her moneybag and pulled the drawstring closed tightly. To William, she said, "Thank you, sir. Enjoy the jam." She moved farther down the table to talk to another customer and left him to think what he pleased.

Later, the town gossip wandered by Emma's table. It was her nature to leave some juicy news behind wherever she traveled and today she lived up to her reputation. "Have you noticed all these fine young men visiting St. Albans? Quite the gentlemen, I dare say. They have all the gals fanning themselves like a herd of cows in heat." She laughed. "It appears there is a man for everyone, even a pleasantly plump, old married woman. Yesterday, one of them helped me across the street after a horse and wagon nearly bowled me over. Even my husband admitted the man performed a kindly act toward a stranger."

"Nice to hear, Mrs. Hodges." Emma busied herself with adding the last of her product to the table.

"Dear, you need to set your sights on the future. Whoever will help your father with the farm when this horrid war is over?"

"Don't you worry about us. Papa and I will manage fine."

She patted Emma's hand. "Of course you will, dear, but it doesn't hurt to look around. Town is oozing with fresh selections—and I don't mean the produce you have for sale."

Emma breathed a sigh of relief when the next captive prey pranced by and the woman abruptly turned to converse with her. At one o'clock in the afternoon, Emma was near starved and lifted a sandwich from the lunchbox she'd packed – white bread smeared with the same jam William purchased. As she bit into it, she envisioned him sitting across the table from her at the farmhouse, the easy talks they'd shared while he recovered, his spontaneous thoughtfulness, protection, but mostly his willingness to suffer pain while rescuing her father from his near-fate. She'd never met a man like him. Yet, he continued to support his band of men that outwardly said and did all the right things to win a person's favor, but inwardly, made her skin crawl. Mama always declared, *A man is known by the friends he keeps company with. Look at them and you will see his true colors.* William was not displaying great character by his choice today.

"Daughter, do you need a break? I will man your table while you stretch your legs for a spell," Joseph said.

Emma jumped from the stump she'd used as a seat. "Thank you, Papa. I saw you cleaning your stall. The elite of St. Albans scooped up all your furniture. If farming ever fails, you can go into the carpentry business."

Joseph laughed. "That would take the fun out of it. Off with you, now."

Emma walked around the Village Green common area in the center of town. She loved the rich hue of the grassland the groundskeeper kept in immaculate condition. The pond lured her to the far side where horses, mules, pigs and sheep littered the space, pining for sips of water while awaiting their fates at the selling tables. Men loitered there, talking and smoking, so she detoured the crowd and ended up on North Main Street facing the Tremont House. It stood a regal five stories high and sufficiently lavish to satisfy the most delicate of clientele. She noticed the scoundrel Bennett Yonge sitting under the grand porch entertaining Mary. William was not with him, and she sighed. What did it matter? She'd sent him from her house and life this morning.

A voice from behind startled her. "Miss Miller, may I walk with you?"

She turned, and the persuasive smile on William's face stole the initial denial that she now silenced. How fickle she'd become. "I suppose it wouldn't hurt to have an escort, with all the people in town today."

William took her arm through his and they started down the street in the other direction.

Streets criss-crossed through town and she felt today that she could do them all while drifting on a cloud. Walking with William, who to everyone that passed them by would see as a brazen act, was probably not the best way to protect one's reputation. But oh, how people would talk if they knew he'd stayed in the privacy of her home for days and that she'd kissed him in the shadow of the woods. The secret made her smile. Yet, what did etiquette matter anymore? Wartime threw protocol and normality out the window like yesterday's wash-water.

"I need to ride hard tonight and I require an alibi. Can I say that you and your father invited me to the farm for dinner and a game of chess?"

Emma glanced at William nervously. "Why would I do that? Better still, who are you expecting to come asking after you at the hill farm?"

"Just want to cover my bases. I need to meet with someone up country."

His face looked earnest enough but the eyes that held the secrets scared Emma. "Up as in Canada, where you hail from?"

"The less you know the better, Emma. Can I count on you?"

"I suppose it wouldn't hurt. We're having leftover rabbit stew."

"Sounds delicious."

"Don't be ridiculous. I'm sick of rabbit, and leftovers are never delicious. When this war is over, I swear I will toss them all in the garbage and never succumb to yesterday's menu again."

"You're angry, and it's not about food," William said.

"If you must know, yes, I am angry. You play the mysterious man who drops in and out of my life, and expects far too much loyalty from a lady on the opposite side of the battlefield."

"Perhaps. But Kentucky is neutral, remember? In fact, they're working with the Union to win the war as we speak."

"That means nothing for the men who signed to ride with the Confederacy."

"Except that this cursed war will be over soon,

the writing is on the wall. The Union will prevail and the Confederates will crawl home with their tail between their legs like lost puppies not knowing how to move forward in the new world."

Emma watched him with interest. "Such deep observations for a man on the losing side."

"I've met lots of men who switched sides," William whispered.

Emma looked at him intently and saw the pleading in his eyes. "You'd likely say anything to win my favor back. But it won't work. I'm reconsidering James as my prime candidate for marriage."

"That would be your choice, Emma. Just know you will break my heart and condemn me to live single the rest of my days."

Emma could not hold back the grin. "Rubbish. Those Southern gals will flock to you like a mother bird to her nest, begging for you to rescue them from the new life of drudgery devoid of slave labor that in the past, pampered their spoiled lives."

"Exactly why I will steer clear of such females. I prefer the hardworking Northern girl who's captured my heart."

They'd walked a while before Emma stopped. "I have shopping to do, William. I think we should part ways now so you can crawl back to your buddies and do whatever it is you do. All your fretting about trouble today has amounted to nothing. As far as I can see, the men who accompanied you have conducted themselves as perfect gentlemen."

"Don't relax your guard, Emma. The war's not over yet." He bent close and whispered, "I'd love to kiss you right now but it shall have to wait until after the rabbit stew."

She watched him walk away, confused whether he was coming to supper or if the invitation had been a decoy to keep Yonge off his trail. His steps appeared heavy, and she wondered if her head and her heart would ever come to an agreement concerning William Davis.

Chapter 11

CONFUSED

Emma awoke to the sound of pebbles tapping against her bedroom window. She'd not closed her curtains and noted it was still dark outside, except for the light from a full moon spilling into her room. She grabbed the top cover and wrapped it around her body, hurrying to the window. She peeked from the side so as not to fully display herself and saw the lone figure on the ground below. It was William. He was diligent if nothing else. She moved to the middle and pushed open the window.

"What are you doing, William Davis?"

"I needed to see you one last time. Is there any rabbit stew left?"

Emma grinned. "I saved you a plate."

"Would you welcome a tired man weary from travel to your table at this hour, Miss Miller?"

"Anything for the war effort. Can't have God's appointed soldiers starving on my doorstep, now can I?"

Emma moved away and lit a lantern. She hurried into a full-length cotton overdress that tied conveniently at the front and pulled on cozy knit slippers. Out of habit she reached for her gun, but at the touch of the cold steel, drew back and left it on the night table. She'd not need that tonight.

Once downstairs, she unbolted the front door and William dashed inside, shivering and wiping the dirt from his boots on the braided mat.

"Come to the kitchen and I'll stir the fire," Emma said.

He sat at the table and she brought him a cup of warm water from the reservoir and added a lemon rind. "I'll put some coffee on."

"Can you make it tea? Sort of missing it tonight."

"Sure—easier for me, and the coffee will remain fresh for Papa in the morning. He'll never know of my midnight visitor."

William reached for her hand.

"Emma, everything will be all right now. You can rest easy; that which man plans for evil will be brought into the light."

"I'm glad your trip was successful—I think." Emma retrieved his plate from the oven and uncovered it. When she plunked it in front of him, he smothered a laugh.

"I thought you were kidding about the rabbit."

Emma's spirit rejuvenated with the sound of his laughter. "I rarely mislead the guests that sit around my table, sir."

Emma watched him down the helping in five minutes flat. She cut a large piece of custard pie and placed it in front of him beside a cup of hot black tea.

"My stomach thanks you, Emma. You are a blessing. Some might have closed the curtain and gone back to bed."

"Some may have, but not me."

"Emma, I realize all this uncertainty is causing a rift between us, but I promise it will get better. And I beg you to watch for my return. I will fight the battle for your hand against James."

Emma bit her lip. "Such gallantry. How will a woman decide?"

He stood, pulling her to her feet. "Maybe this will help."

He kissed her again, and she melted against him. "My heart betrays me," Emma said.

"Mine will lead me back to you." He kissed the top of her head and pushed away. "Now I must sneak into my room at the hotel and go about business as usual tomorrow. Stay home and stay safe."

The next morning, Emma forgot about his advice when her father spilled all his hard-earned coins on the table. She dumped hers from the drawstring purse, and together it grew into a heap of money, enough to see them through the winter months.

"The Good Lord has provided again, daughter." He scooped a small amount into the money jar in the cupboard before he spoke. "Take the rest to town, Emma, and tuck it safely in the bank account to use on a rainy day. Take Ethan's horse—she's yours now. No need to walk."

In the barn, Emma spoke in a soothing voice to her deceased brother's horse, Blaze, as she saddled her. The animal appeared content to exchange ownership from Ethan to her, likely preferring anything to riding through forests and streams in the thick of battle and smelling the constant stench of death. With the task completed, she fastened the money pouch tightly around her waist and let it dangle unseen beneath the folds of her dress. Emma took hold of the lead rope and walked Blaze into the barnyard before attempting to mount her for the first time, wondering if the animal would accept her as the new owner. Blaze welcomed her with a gentle whinny as she hooked the handle of the egg basket carrying her meager half-dozen eggs over the horn on the saddle before she mounted. The laying hens were taking a well-deserved break for she'd cleaned them out yesterday for the sale, but she'd sell these few at the mercantile.

The sky exposed a mix of sun and clouds but continued to shed a blanket of warmth despite the changing season. Orange, red and gold leaves from oaks and maples scattered loosely and their crunch under the horse's hooves broke the silence of the day. Gusts of wind lifted the weightless foliage and rattled it across the path in front of her. She glanced toward the mountain peaks of the Adirondacks and saw the telltale white beginning to form. Today, the weather still allowed her to wear a wool cape, but all too soon, she'd require her heavy coat and boots.

Emma rounded the last corner, and St. Albans loomed before her. The first glimpse of her hometown never failed to bring back the beginning of it all – when the birth of war fever infected every man that drew breath. She allowed her mind to drift as she steered Blaze toward Statford's Mercantile.

Emma recalled the patriotic spirit that had captured the community when Governor Fairbanks received a telegram from the new President, Abraham Lincoln, pleading for Vermont to send funds and soldiers. After the slave-holding states won a Republican victory, they'd withdrawn from the Union. War was on the horizon. Vermonters responded to their president by doing their *full duty* – no one suspecting the degrading depths awaiting them. Sending money to help sustain the U.S. national government and support the war effort proved the least important *duty* in Emma's eyes, when compared to the gravestones that now littered the countryside.

They'd sent the best of their men. Emma's eldest brother Mason, had marched with the first regiment of seven hundred and eighty-two soldiers to suppress the rebellion in April 1861. These first troops took pride in attaching a hemlock sprig to their caps in remembrance of the Green Montana Boys of the American Revolution. But in ninety days, after seeing only one battle on the Virginia Peninsula, the Rebels claimed victory at Big Bethel. Mason never returned home.

The 2nd Vermont regiment enlisted for three years, joining the Army of the Potomac, the largest of all Union armies. Emma had falsely concluded that great numbers had the power to keep soldiers safe, but on July 21st the second Miller brother Henry, fought in the battle at Bull Run and died head down in the stream with a bullet in his chest. Emma begged her youngest brother Ethan not to enlist, but after Mama's death, his conscience grew heavy, and he joined James in the battle. One short year ago, she'd watched him march off to his death. Her family destroyed in just over a three-year period. The future looked bleak for the Miller Hillside Farm with only she and her father left standing. Would the end of the war usher in the annihilation of the entire Miller legacy? She shivered at the thought of being wiped from the pages of history, as if her family never existed.

Emma shook her head free of such negative thoughts. Many hoped for the coming Union victory—her included. The fight against slavery was a noble cause, but the hardships that followed the first cannon shot instigated a downward spiral that no one had dreamed possible. The Union to the North and the Confederacy of the Southern states collided, headstrong and determined to have their way concerning tariffs, trade and state rights. But for St. Albans, slavery was the issue nearest and dearest to their hearts and many unnamed Vermonters risked their lives transporting slaves through the Underground Railroad.

For the most part, St Albans remained a peaceable town, enduring few skirmishes and outbreaks from the opposition. The greatest disappointments came when Union renegade bands pressed through and demanded more from the

Northerners than they should. The war changed people and trust was a rare commodity. The townsfolk learned the hard way to shield themselves from realities they could not hope to understand. Day after day, the population went about their business, lifting silent prayers for the safe return of loved ones and an end to a war that had lasted far too long.

Emma tied her mount to the hitching post and walked inside. Mr. Statford's eager voice greeted her. "Why, Emma Miller? Back so soon. Yesterday's festivities provided a wonderful get-together for everyone, and it didn't hurt that the crowds came in from miles around with money burning holes in their pockets. Did you profit from selling your wares in the Commons?"

"I did. I'll be depositing it in the bank today for safe keeping. Papa told me to spend some on myself so I'll be donning a new hairstyle next time I see you. I have a few eggs for the store today."

She threw back the cover, and the proprietor whistled. "I swear you have the best laying hens in the whole county."

"I give thanks for Gertrude and her gang of hens every day," Emma said.

"Do you have any shopping to do today?" he asked as he removed each one and laid them carefully in a special container he'd rigged up. He then placed them safely inside the glass cabinet for his customers to view prior to purchasing.

"I made a list. Can I come back this afternoon after a late luncheon with Mary? Told Papa I'd be home in time to get supper on the table."

"No problem. Take all the time you need. You work far too hard for such a young girl."

Outside Emma walked at a leisurely pace, peering in the storefronts and dreaming. She did not see Bennett Yonge until he slithered up beside her.

"Afternoon, Miss Miller. William was sure bragging up last night's dinner out at your place. Don't know what he sees in a country bumpkin, but to each his own. Had my fill last night too, I believe Mary is her name. Oh, yes, she's a friend of yours, right?"

Emma gasped. She did not like the way he leered with satisfaction and prayed Mary possessed sense enough not to bring disgrace upon her name with this despicable man.

"Yeah, that's about the same response she had—after the fact. Couldn't get her to stop crying so I walked out. Northern gals are so confusing."

"Stay away from me, Mr. Yonge." Emma picked up the pace. His quickened, and he soon caught up.

"Now that's not friendly." He rambled on and Emma wished she could somehow block out his boasting spirit. "Reckon I'll have my pick of gals back home. And I'll build the lucky one the finest house in Kentucky. My folks would prefer me bringing a rich one home but I prefer ones from the poor side of town, if you know what I mean. They know how to give a man what he needs, not like the uppity-frigid Southern gals that swoon when you try to steal a kiss." Yonge laughed. "Hey, since Will doesn't want his little redhead, maybe she'll take a shine to me. That will set him on his heels when he comes running back after he's had his fill of you."

"I am not interested in your romantic exploits, Mr. Yonge." Emma ground to a halt. "Safe travels and goodbye." She disappeared inside The Jan-Mor Beauty Shop and shut the door firmly behind her. She watched as he made his way to the American House where William stayed, undoubtedly full of new gossip to spread.

"Good riddance to the both of you," she muttered, while wiping a tear from her eye.

Chapter 12

ST. ALBANS RAID

By the time Emma entered Robinson's Diner, ominous clouds darkened the sky threatening a downpour. Mary chatted casually as they finished up a late lunch, Emma grateful that the subject of her friend's whereabouts last night never entered the conversation.

Suddenly, the door swung open, and along with the clientele that entered, boisterous laughter followed them in from outside. The noise carried clear passed through the front row of tables to where the ladies sat. Emma peered out the window. Across from the American House, Yonge created a lively scene, and the commotion was attracting a growing crowd.

"What do you suppose is going on over there?" Emma asked.

Mary tracked the direction of her stare. "Drat—I was hoping you and I could take a walk over there before the rain forced you home," Mary said.

"Do you not wonder what's happening?" Emma asked.

"Think I recognize a few of them. They were in Bennett's hotel room yesterday."

Shocked by her open confession, Emma said. "Did you know he wasted no time in bragging that he had his way with you?"

"He did not! The man is all talk. He honored my refusal toward his advances and gave me leave. Of course, on the way out, I made a grand fool of myself by tripping and falling flat on my face. The tears I shed helped aid my departure. I don't think he enjoyed seeing that side of a woman."

"At least he was right about the tears," Emma said.

"Surely you didn't suspect I'd fall prey to his silver tongue?"

Pink flushed across Emma's face, embarrassed that she'd believed his boast. "I'm sorry. The man knows how to goad me. I'm relieved you stood strong."

"But those fellas loafing over there would not have backed down. They're a bad lot. I locked my door last night and pushed a table across it in case any came calling. I should never have let Bennett bring me up. But I could never afford to stay in a place as grand as the Tremont and let my curiosity get the better of me."

"Well, I'm more curious in what's happening out there right now." Emma stood to her feet. The women tossed money on the table, gathered their belongings, and stepped outside.

The slight breeze carried the voices to Emma's ears. Yonge continued to shout in his typical braggart style. The man was all about putting on a show.

"I take possession of this town in the name of the Confederate States of America," Yonge proclaimed outside the American House. He repeated the declaration that he was "going to take the town and shoot the first person to resist". At first the bystanders thought it was all a staged joke, but when gunfire and Rebel yells filled the air, they began to panic.

The church clock chimed at three-o'clock and all chaos erupted.

Bennett Yonge and others armed with pistols began to herd people across Main Street and on to the Village Green. Emma noticed William and cringed.

Mary gasped and pointed to the livery. "Emma, it's Fuller's place!" The pair huddled close to the wall of the building as they watched the bedlam unfold on the streets of St. Albans.

"No! We'll take care of our own horses!" the leader of the group said, while jumping on the back of a stray animal. In haste others followed his lead, helping themselves to geldings and mules from inside the corral.

When Fuller recovered from the commotion, he yelled, "What are you doing? Give back those animals!" A few neighbors joined him, all surprised and gaping at the brazenness of the thieves. "If you don't keep still, I will shoot you!" Fuller threatened.

How could the town fight back? Guns and ammunition were a rare find, as volunteers leaving to fight the good fight had taken most of their meager supply with them, never suspecting the Confederates would spread to the furthermost state in the country to endanger their families. The law had ridden out this morning, and all that remained to defend the village comprised of frightened women, businessmen, and senior residents.

Emma heard the fear in Fuller's voice and the ridiculing laugh of the men now looming over him while perched high on their horses. Emma swallowed hard. Fuller withdrew and returned moments later, this time standing near Mr. Bildad's Shoe Shop. The crazed man aimed a 6-shooter – a poor excuse for a firearm – at the man who'd cussed him. Emma noted the horse thieves wore heavy revolvers strapped to their sides and lifted a hand to stifle her scream that could distract Fuller from concentrating on his tragic predicament. Fuller pulled the trigger three times in a row, for she could hear the horrid click of emptiness in the air.

"What is Fuller thinking?" Emma muttered aloud.

The leader aimed his gun at Fuller, and with dramatic poise, pretended to shoot. They all howled with jeering laughter and more chaos broke out. Random shots fired through the air. Poor Mr. Morrison, the contractor for the new hotel, stood on the steps of Miss Beattie's shop, with his left hand on the latch of the door and his right in the pocket of his coat. A stray bullet, or possibly an intentional one, shot straight through his right hand, likely lodging in his bowel.

The injured man staggered next door to the stairway of the messenger's office groaning, "I'm shot." One hand pressed on his stomach as he buckled. Two men from inside the building raced to help and dragged him into Dutcher and Son's Drug Store. A few minutes later, Emma noticed Doc hurry in behind them.

When the bunch of horses and riders raced

through the street, Mary fled toward her rented room, and Emma ducked inside the bank. From the window she noticed George Conger, some retired Union men, and townsfolk rallying. Emma's attention shifted south to the other end of Main Street. More armed horsemen shooting guns off at odd angles, terrorized the quiet community.

She recognized many of her friends and neighbors standing silent and speechless. The war had come in force to St. Albans, and they were ill prepared for the brutality of it. So preoccupied with the scene outdoors was she that Emma took no notice of the four men who entered St. Albans Bank. She noticed Cyrus Bishop outside, pointing at the window where she stood, yelling warnings and then racing to the back office where Martin Seymour worked.

Emma turned and scanned the interior of the bank to discover four Confederate thieves waving guns in the air and rounding up the patrons to one side of the room. After locking the main door, a whiskered ruffian grabbed Emma's arm and pushed her hard toward the group, landing her in the middle of a heap of bodies on the floor.

The businessmen, dressed in suits with pencils tucked behind their ears, presented little threat for cavalrymen bent on filling their pockets. The raiders quickly pushed through the inner door at the back, the force of hardwood meeting skull, struck Bishop and sent him rolling off balance.

They ordered the newly taken hostages in the office to keep silent. The assailants ranted about exacting vengeance for the plunder Union soldiers had executed in the Shenandoah Valley. And now in St. Albans, the war had come home to roost. Bishop and Seymour sat staring down the barrel of a pistol while greedy men set their sights on the treasures within.

From Emma's location, she could hear and see all that transpired in the backroom. The robbers cracked the bank door, filled kit bags and lined their pockets with bank notes taken from Bishop's table and in the safe. With all the employees and customers herded against the far wall in the main room, the bandits did not once think to check the money-laden drawers under the bank's abandoned counters. At least they'd not get away with that booty, or hers. She felt the bag fastened to the side of her waistline, tucked under multiple layers of material, out of sight from the thieving scoundrels.

One man they called Price screeched like a hawk descending on prey when he hit upon a large bag of silver. But when together the foursome could not carry the treasure, they carefully counted out four hundred dollars, leaving almost four times as much scattered on the floor.

Emma's attention switched to outside the front window. She watched the door from Weatherbee's Gentleman's Furnishing Store open and close. It was five minutes past three and time for Samuel Breck to do his daily deposit. You could run a clock on him, predictable and precise. He appeared distracted with the goings on in the streets and reached for the handle to the door. He turned it and nothing happened. Glancing at the town clock he frowned. The man hated inconvenience of any kind. One raider noticed him and rushed to open the door before he could sound the alarm. Thrusting a gun in Breck's face, he pulled him inside and snarled, "I take deposits."

With a pistol at his head, Breck offered little argument, and after being relieved of his moneybag, went to sit on the floor with the rest. He leaned against the wall beside Emma. "Just lost three hundred and ninety-three dollars to that scum."

While the guard by the door waited for those in the back room to finish, he waylaid a couple more customers in the same manner. Morris Roach was younger than Emma, and she felt sick when he lost two hundred and ten dollars of his employer Joseph Week's, daily profits to the bandit.

A man they called Spurr began to pace in front of the group, lecturing the hostages with a booming voice about General Sheridan and how this day was one of retaliation. Emma doubted that was the real reason for the heist, but it sounded noble and war-worthy. Tomorrow, newspapers would print his exact words for everyone to read. But if the crooks assumed vengeance would somehow validate this horrific raid in St. Albans, they were sadly mistaken.

In the back, Seymour was being his old cantankerous self, who defied anyone to run amuck his finely tuned bank business. He refused to admit if there was gold on the premises and demanded time to take an inventory, saying that if this were truly an act of war, the bank would post a government claim to cover its losses.

Collins rushed in and slapped his mouth with the butt of his gun. "Damn your government, hold up your hands." He then forced the Vermonters, at gunpoint, to "*solemnly swear to obey and respect the Constitution of the Confederate States of America*" and that they would "*not fire on the men of that government in this town*" and further "*they would not report the robbery until two hours later*".

It all sounded bizarre to Emma and before it finished, Collins humiliating episode tickled the ears of his fellow raiders.

"Time's up. It's time to go, Collins," one stated. He waved his gun to the two men still standing with their hands lifted in surrender. "You can lower your hands, men."

The St. Albans Bank heist ended as suddenly as it began. Yonge popped his head inside. "It's over boys. Let's ride." In that fleeting second, his gaze scanned the hostages against the wall and noticed Emma. He laughed. "Now there's a little lady we can

take as a hostage; safe passage 'til we clear the area."
He walked over, grabbed Emma's wrist, and pulled
her to her feet. "We're going to have to stop meeting
like this, Miss Miller."

The raiders began to exit, dragging Emma
along with them. Two remained a moment longer
than the others – pointing pistols at the employees as
they backed out the door.

Chapter 13

THE HOSTAGE

Tears threatened to escape Emma's eyes. Where was William? Frustration overwhelmed her. Sadly outnumbered, what could he possibly do? She expected too much from the Confederate soldier who followed orders to stay alive. The whole heist took under fifteen minutes and she sickened at the memory of wonder-lust she'd seen for the prize weighing down their hands.

"Leave the girl," Spurr shouted.

"No way. She's our ticket out of here." Something akin to vengeance ate at Yonge, leaving Emma uncertain whether it targeted William or her.

Bennett Yonge pushed Emma out the door ahead of him. Men on horses stood waiting and after throwing his bag to someone, he slung his legs over his horse and reached down for her. She hesitated. He bent low and said, "I can still make it hard for lover boy back in Kentucky – if he makes it that far. Hop up here before I lose my patience."

Emma did not expect the arm that reached out and literally pulled her onto the horse's back, forcing her to hang on for dear life. He kicked the animal and joined the exiting rioters who demanded center stage as the curtain fell on the closing act of their treachery. Random shots from the burglars blazed in all directions, celebrating a huge haul.

As the street scene swirled through Emma's line of vision, she observed some citizens speechless while crouching beside buildings for support, women and children running inside for cover and men scratching their heads in bewilderment. The surprise attack held the community powerless to react.

Out of the corner of her eye, she noticed the manager run from the bank screaming so loud even Emma atop the twirling horse could make out the words. "The bank's been robbed! What shall we do?"

Another businessman, Carnie, came running and added to the dilemma. "Not just this one—they've cleaned out all the banks!"

When a bullet grazed Carnie's head, landing

in the post beyond his ear, both men disappeared inside the nearest building.

At least twenty, maybe more littered the road, hollering and shooting bullets into the air. The plan had taken place simultaneously and left the inhabitants of St. Albans exasperated, standing in a muddle of chaos. Strange what passes through a mind amid such madness. It was all the disconnected things; Mary—had she made it home safely? Papa—was he watching for her return? William—had he helped to rob the other banks? And why did her heart continue to flip-flop over a disappointing romance? More than anything Emma wanted to believe in William, but the cards were stacked against him.

The sudden appearance of George Conger interrupted her disjointed thoughts. The retired soldier wore his dark blue frock coat and forage cap from the days he'd served as a Union captain in the Vermont Cavalry. She peered beyond him and discovered he galloped alone, riding frantically up and down the street while swinging his bayonet and yelling the obvious, "Rebel raiders are upon us. Arm yourself people, with anything—even broomsticks."

Surely he saw the terror was no longer on the ground, and that a man without a horse and gun would not stop this team of robbers from leaving town with the loot. George acted on pure adrenalin and she wondered if any good would come from his ranting.

Bennett Yonge reared his horse. Emma bit off a scream and with white-knuckled fingers, gripped his coat tighter. She considered slipping to the ground, free at last from this vile man, but fear of being trampled by the stampede of horses kept her seated.

Yonge, the Lieutenant of the Confederate thieves, yelled to his men and circled his arms repeatedly in the air to wind up the show they'd displayed for the Northerners. "Time to leave, boys. We've worn out our welcome."

As Emma passed George, their eyes met briefly, and she noted the startled look on his face. He'd inform James the moment he had the chance, but in her heart of hearts, she desired her rescue to come from William Davis, not James. *Trust.* He'd asked her to trust him. Did the happenings of life all boil down to trust? She contemplated God's purpose in this strange kidnapping and petitioned a higher source, for He undoubtedly deserved her complete trust.

The band of thieves headed northwest, racing down the same dirt road she'd arrived on earlier. Emma heard the hoofbeats behind her but focused on staying upright on the fast galloping animal. Trees whizzed by. Dizziness overwhelmed her as thick fog hung in the air from the threatening weather that had not yet released its fury. Yonge lifted his arm and waved for the soldiers to follow him into the woods. It slowed their progress, and she wondered why they headed toward the lake. Twigs pierced and slashed at her arms, and she was grateful for the protective coat she wore. The worn fabric on the cuffs of her dress did not handle the thrashing long, and soon the frayed hems dripped with blood from cuts slicing the little skin that showed.

Emma pounded on his back. "Slow down, you lunatic."

In return, she heard ridicule in his tone. "Welcome to the war, Miss Miller."

"A war of your own making. You are a sorry excuse for a military officer."

"I can see what our Willy likes about you— you are right sassy." He licked his lips and she backed off, holding his coattail and keeping as far from his back as she could manage without tumbling to the ground.

When they reached an open section bordering Lake Champlain, Yonge threw his arm in the air and the troops barely slowed before wheeling their horses to a stop. With the speed of a plan in motion, men dismounted. Emma scanned the group frantically.

"Who you looking for?" Yonge asked.

"No one," she lied.

"Smiley will join us soon. You remember him – one of the boys who wanted you to cook breakfast for him in town?" His laugher filled with mockery.

"He jumped off the trail back a spell—seems he had some unfinished business to tend to."

"William?" Emma cried. She regrouped her thoughts, forcing the pleading tone to silence while she attempted reason. "I understood Mr. Davis was your childhood friend?"

"Favorites don't play out well with this lot." He reached for her hand. "Get off the horse."

"Why are you stopping? The Union will soon be on your trail," Emma said.

"I'm shaking in my boots," one of the men said before doubling over with amusement.

"Gotta' watch those old ladies with their straw brooms, boys."

"Grown men carrying peashooters that wouldn't hurt a fly."

"Town was a few Yankee Doodle Dandies short for protecting their treasury, I'd say."

The men roared as each one took turns ridiculing the response from the people of St. Albans. These strangers spoke ill of her neighbors, George, and the Union. Emma realized it would be a while before they formed a posse to rescue her. Tears gathered in the corners of her eyes and she turned away.

Yonge noticed and said, "Embarrassed to call

them your own kind?"

"Not for a minute! Honor is their sword and God is their hope. I have never in my entire life met such despicable creatures as the ones who invaded my home soil today."

"Whoopie—that lady should run for office," someone shouted.

Yonge pointed to a tree. "Wait over there."

"What am I waiting for?" Emma asked with a boldness that boiled from within.

"None of your business. Just sit and shut up."

A short distance off, the men gathered in a circle and opened the loot bags. Heaps of paper money, coins, and documents from three banks spilled onto the ground. When the hollering subsided, Yonge sat in the middle and grinned.

"We need twenty-six equal piles—twenty-five for us and one lonely stack to help replenish the Confederate treasury. And we need to do it quick. Let's get to counting boys."

They all cheered then silence swept over the robbers as the mounds grew. Inside Emma cried for the hard-working business owners, farmers, ranchers and trappers, as she witnessed their lost profits lying on soiled ground while greedy men divided the plunder. Hers remained hidden, and she almost felt guilty that she'd never deposited it in the bank earlier, so she could share in the loss with her neighbors.

After a few minutes, Yonge stood and stretched. "Nature calling. Be right back, gents. Get ready to ride. Only twelve miles and we'll cross the Canadian border." He disappeared into the woods. Men started stashing their booty in knapsacks, preparing to pull out.

Emma startled as she heard a whisper close to her ear. "Do you know where you are, little miss? Just nod; don't speak."

She recognized Yonge's voice behind her and nodded yes. Did they honestly think they'd lose her in her own backyard? She'd played in these woods her entire life.

"Behind the tree you'll find William's stash— enough to give you two a fresh start if Smiley doesn't finish him off first. Tell him it's payment for an old debt and that I hope he makes it through the war. When we cross paths again, the war will be history and we'll all be rich men." He took a deep breath. "Yeah, and tell him thanks for the Southern-bred redhead. She was always meant to be mine."

All fell silent and within the moment, Yonge wandered out of the bush. He grabbed two piles that remained on the ground and packed his horse. He flung his body overtop in one easy sweep and yelled to his men. "Every man for himself. Good luck. See you back in America, after the victory flag is raised high." He tipped his head to Emma. "Enjoy the walk home, Miss Miller. Mighty glad you could join us for the afternoon."

With the lure of money tucked in saddle packs, no leering soldier seemed interested in staying behind to torment Emma, and for that she was grateful. Her small gun still lay deep inside her pocket, but gratitude flooded her in the knowledge she'd not have to kill a man today. She sat by the tree until the last rider snuck off through the woods, raced down the main road, or boarded a small vessel stowed in the brushes nearby. Surely, they'd arrive safely in Canada before George rounded up a group big enough to give chase. She exhaled deeply with regret, for she could do nothing to stop them.

Emma wondered about the outcome—if the neighboring country would welcome the Confederates or stand with Lincoln and hang them as traitors. But what did that matter to the farm girl who lost everything? Even William. Since that one brief glimpse in St. Albans, the man had disappeared.

Emma staggered to her feet and forced her cramped body to move. Even nature rejoiced in the absence of evil, for the birds chirped again, and the squirrels scampered from hiding to continue their quest for winter feed. Her ears fixed on the sounds of a horse. She rounded a bush by the lake and wept openly. Of all the horses stolen in town, the thief who'd taken Blaze had chosen to travel by water to

Canada. Considering this unexpected miracle, Emma's faith multiplied.

The sun had set in the western sky by the time she reached the laneway to the farmhouse. Emma lingered to drink in the beauty of the crimson sky and relish the promise of fair weather tomorrow. The threat of rain had passed by without dumping its fury and she'd remained dry and warm. Exhausted physically, she craved to relax in a warm bath and rest before facing the next adventure life had in store.

Emma swung Blaze toward the barn, and the closer she drew, the quicker she galloped, as if home would disappear before she reached its shelter behind familiar walls. Stripped of his saddle, Blaze enjoyed a quick brush. The animal pushed at her, eager to indulge in the fresh hay and water Papa had placed in the feeder. Emma closed the barn doors and hurried toward the house. She quickened her pace, dashed up the porch steps, and flung open the door, slamming it shut and collapsing against it. She threw the money burden—William's take in the robbery—into the corner, and after bolting the entry, headed for the kitchen.

When she entered, Emma stopped dead in her tracks. It appeared Jed was in cahoots with Smiley in the goal to seek revenge against William and her, for the man stretched in a laid back position on a chair, his feet resting on the kitchen table.

Chapter 14

RETURNING HOME

Emma gasped at the sudden vulnerability of her situation as she watched his face darken with evil intent. She remembered the gun and slipped her hand into her pocket. If he attempted anything, she'd have to shoot him in her own kitchen. Would the horror never end?

He let the legs of the chair fall back on the floor. "Well, aren't you a sight for tired eyes? Been waiting for the boys to swing by and pick me up."

"You'll be waiting a long time. They are halfway to Canada by now."

The man jumped to his feet. "You're lying!"

"Not at all. They kidnapped me, dumped me by the lake, and I rode home."

"What about my share of the loot?"

Hoping to escape the man, Emma lied. "Bennett Yonge told me he has your booty and will meet you in Canada."

Jed spit on the floor. "Canada's a big country."

She bit her tongue. "I'm sure you remember the hangouts."

He began to pace and Emma elected to hurry his decision along. "Can I pack you a quick lunch? If you hurry, you might catch up."

"I don't need food. Been cleaning up leftovers for a couple hours now."

"Then God's speed to you, sir." She wished she had the courage to aim her gun at him and bring him to St. Albans to receive the justice he deserved, but fear gripped her heart, and getting rid of him was her preferred choice. Let the Union chase him.

"You'd like that, wouldn't you?" Emma witnessed the hesitation in his face. "How do I know you're telling the truth?"

"Why would I lie?"

"To save yourself from my taking pleasure with you."

Emma noticed his guns and bayonet leaning against the far wall. If she would ever attempt option number two, it needed to be now. She took a deep breath and withdrew the gun from her pocket and aimed it at Jed.

"Sit down, soldier." When he glanced toward his weapons, she raised her voice. "Now!" As Emma moved closer, she stopped by a drawer and withdrew a spool of strong, tightly bound rope she'd purchased to use as a clothesline. "Put your hands behind your back." This would be the tricky part. Could she tie him without him overtaking her? She was strong and God was on her side. "Push your chair against that centre beam out in the open."

"You know how to use that thing?"

"Killed many an animal. You're the sorriest of the lot."

A sly grin came over his face. "I know what you're up to. If you tie me up, you can have your way with me. I know what a woman wants."

Inside she wanted to vomit, but she'd play into his stupidity if it meant securing him with knots against the unmovable post.

"My, aren't you the smart one?"

"Knew you'd get sick of William." He moved into position. "Come on, woman, I don't have all day. Got me some hard riding ahead."

Emma moved in behind the now cooperative man and pulled his hands around the back of the chair and the post. It was a good stretch, and he grunted. "Not too comfy for me, sweetheart, but we'll have it your way." She knew how to tie a secure knot and laid her gun on the floor for the final tug. Retrieving it again, she walked to the front to face her prisoner. He responded with a "Whoopee!" and she smiled. The fool.

The smell of strong coffee filled the air, and she made her way to the stove. Emma poured herself a cup and sat at the table staring out the window.

"What are you doing?" Jed asked.

"Trying to figure out how long we'll have to wait before the Union comes calling to see if I'm all right."

"What?" The man seemed surprised and again the word *fool* toyed at her mind. Were all men stupid or just Graybacks?

"Keep quiet or I'll gag you, and it won't be for your pleasure, sir."

Jed cussed and called her an unbecoming name that she'd only heard from drunkards addressing the bargirls inside saloons as she passed by. The females in that establishment hadn't minded the disrespect, but the crudeness did not sit well with Emma. She grabbed a piece of stale bread left over from this morning's breakfast that still lay littered on the counter. She smeared butter and raspberry jam on the top and sighed. Her kitchen was the dirtiest she'd ever seen it and would take days of scrubbing to clear the stench and memory of the Confederate invasion of her home.

"You don't like us, do you?"

"We are all God's creatures. May He have mercy on your soul."

"Never had time for church."

"You should take the time now and talk to Him. Give my ears a rest," Emma said.

"William is one of us and you'll never make a Northerner out of him. He's drenched and spoiled in Southern comfort."

When she didn't answer, he continued. "Got your father tied and gagged upstairs. Would have shot him, but he looks too much like my old man so I figured I'd give him a break."

"And I will do likewise, if you don't shut up," Emma said. The threat of restraint did not stop the flow.

"Smiley's taking care of your sweetheart. I wouldn't be expecting him back anytime soon."

"And they assigned you to me? How lucky for you." Emma said. "You should have ridden off with the others while you had the chance."

"Had me a job to finish. But it looks like Yonge played me for a fool, dragged you off with him. Willy and the lieutenant have gnawed at each other about women the whole time I've known them. Think it's an old skirmish from their days in Kentucky. Surprised that he let you go."

"A pocket full of money gives a man new perspective. Too bad you hadn't taken the bait. You'd be riding free by now."

"You think you have the upper hand, don't you?" Jed laughed. "Smiley's still out there and he won't desert me. And when he cuts me loose—and he will—you'll experience firsthand a man's vengeance."

Emma stood and walked into her medical room. She came out with a long strip of white bandage and smiled. "I've heard enough" and gagged him.

Next, she went upstairs and untied her father. He was spitting mad, but she filled him in on the details of her day and concern replaced the anger.

"I sent you to town. It's all my fault you were there," Joseph said.

Emma took the small moneybag from its hiding place, shook it in the air until the coins jingled then smiled. "Never got to deposit yesterday's money."

Joseph roared laughing. "Well, the jokes on them. Riding with a hostage carrying a purse full. Sorry excuse for thieves, aren't they?"

Emma placed the bag on the dresser. "Come downstairs. Coffee's on, and you can get reacquainted with Jed, Yonge's cook—remember?"

"I remember."

Emma fussed, cleaning the kitchen of all signs of today's disorder. Emma wiped her hands clean and heard a rider approaching. Darkness had fallen, but moonlight dispelled the shadows. She lit a second lantern and went to the front door. Heavy feet pounded up the steps, and she peeked out the smaller window to the side of the main entrance.

William's familiar face met hers as he passed by. Thank God. She unbolted the door and without hesitation, flew into his arms. He buried his hands in the loose braids at the back of her neck and pulled her close, repeating her name, like music in her ears. She snuggled in and extracted all the comfort his arms offered. He smelled of sweat and saddle grease but pure joy in seeing him alive and on her doorstep masked the offensive odor.

"Smiley?" Emma asked.

"Not our problem. George will lock him in the town jailhouse. Sheriff can deal with him when he returns."

"I have his friend tied up in the kitchen. So glad you came along to clean up my mess."

"Jed—in the kitchen?"

"Tied up and ready for transport to jail."

"And your father?"

"Fine. Keeping watch and emptying the coffee pot."

He grinned at Emma. "I believe I've snagged myself an independent woman."

"And growing stronger by the minute. If this war continues much longer, you may never recognize the meek farm girl who stole your heart."

"Meek? I missed that part." William laughed. "That little-girl look never fooled me for a minute. My image of the strong, young woman I've grown to love replaced any helplessness I felt in seeing you ride out of town on the back of Bennett's horse. But, when we caught up, I glimpsed Yonge's back and noticed you gone. That's when I panicked. George told me to come look for you. With Canada alerted, and a posse of fifty from St. Albans, I figured they didn't need me anymore." William chuckled. "It was quite the spectacle—your townsfolk; some in buggies, carrying clubs and shovels, anything they could lay their hands on quickly."

"You rode with the Union today?"

"I recall telling you that some soldiers switched sides."

"But you led me to believe…"

"Shush, my love. Few will ever know of my involvement in this whole venture. Spying is a lonely existence, Emma. But both our lives depended on the Confederates believing I was who they thought I was, so I continued the farce."

"I'll know, and St. Albans will know. That will be enough."

"That is a definite plus if I plan to settle in these parts."

"And do you?" Emma asked. "An ex-spy filled with secrets?"

"We will have a lifetime to uncover them all. That is, if you'll have me, Emma Miller?"

"Is this another feeble attempt at a marriage proposal, Mr. Davis?"

He grinned. "I see even a Northern farm girl likes to experience all the fuss of a man on his knees."

William dropped to the floor and took her left hand in his, kissing it long and soft. His eyes lifted and his heart spoke as loudly as his words. "Emma Miller, will you do me the honor of becoming my wife?"

She grinned. "I thought you'd never ask."

THE END

Let's Stay Connected

Check out all her historical and contemporary books here:

https://www.amazon.com/-/e/B00J9RM116

Join readers on FB at Dream Creations: Romance fans

https://www.facebook.com/groups/1118008614903688/

Sign up for her newsletter: New releases & books deals.

http://eepurl.com/djNqjn

Subscribe to her website:

marlenebierworth.com

**IF you enjoyed this book, I would appreciate you returning to the sales page where you purchased this book and leaving a short helpful review to inspire other readers to consider this book. Thank you for your help in this matter.

Author's Bio

Dream Creations: bringing words of hope for the nations. Marlene writes Christian romance books, both historical and contemporary, with a twist of mystery, adventure, suspense and drama to set your pulse racing. She is a wife, mother, grandmother and follower of Jesus.

More Books in the
War Time Romance Collection Series:

1.Oregon Bride

2.Vermont Bride

Made in the USA
Middletown, DE
02 February 2022

60284548R00097